Spies Dad, Big Lauren & Me

Joanna Nadin is a former journalist and government speechwriter. She has written several award-winning books for younger readers, as well as the best-selling Rachel Riley series for teens. She lives in Bath with her daughter.

Visit www.joannanadin.com to find out more.

Spies, Dad, Big Lauren & Me

Joanna Nadin

Piccadilly Press • London

First published in Great Britain in 2011
by Piccadilly Press Ltd,
5 Castle Road, London NW1 8PR
www.piccadillypress.co.uk

Text copyright © Joanna Nadin, 2011

A catalogue record for this book is available from the British Library

ISBN: 978 1 84812 122 5 (paperback)

1 3 5 7 9 10 8 6 4 2

Printed in the UK by CPI Bookmarque Ltd, Croydon, CR1 4PD
Cover design by Simon Davis
Cover illustrations by Sarah Kelly

When I Grow Up
by Billy Grimshaw

When I grow up I want to be a spy, like Zac Black, or my dad. Zac Black is a secret agent with superpowers and special gadgets and he's in four books, three films and a TV series and was my dad's favourite when he was my age.

My dad's already a spy. Except he doesn't have superpowers like x-ray vision, or a laser beam biro. But I know he's a spy because last time I saw him, which was on Boxing Day when he picked me and my brother Stan up to see Granny Grimshaw, he was always on his mobile saying things like, 'The big cheese says just one more week and then it's all over,' which is exactly what Zac Black said in the episode when he caught his mortal enemy Dr Van Fleet trying to poison the water supply in New York with truth serum. Plus that's why Dad lives in London now, so he can be closer to MI5. I haven't been to London yet, but I know what it's like. I've seen it on TV. Everyone lives in loft apartments, which is where everything is in one room. Except for the toilet because that would be disgusting having to see someone poo while you're watching *Millionaire*, for instance. I'm going to go and stay there soon. Mum's checking a weekend with him when he's not too busy (i.e. at MI5 headquarters). Stan says he's not going because he'll miss *Doctor Who*, but he's mad because they have *Doctor Who* in London, and anyway Mum can record it. Mum says Dad moved to London because he got a job on a bigger newspaper than the *Broadley Echo*, but that's just his cover. All spies have a cover story. Like Zac Black pretends to go to work every day at Global Bank but instead of going up to the third floor where the bank is, he goes down to the basement which is his headquarters, and uses his supersonic sonar radar and his x-ray vision to track down Dr Van Fleet and his minion Vespa Morris.

I'm already training to be a spy. I've got binoculars, and a *James Bond* box set and the *Zac Black Annual 1985*, which has the Top Ten Tips for Junior Spies. I don't have a mortal enemy yet, but I'm keeping my eyes peeled, which is Tip Number 5.

On the MI5 website it says you have to be at least eighteen to be an Intelligence Officer, a.k.a. a spy. But, when I'm good enough, Dad will just come and pick me up and I'll be his assistant, like Angelica Drew in *Zac Black*, except not a girl, and we'll live in the loft and have orange juice on a tap in the fridge and beds in the air. Maybe they'll make a TV series about us one day.

Saturday
31st May

Something Bad has happened. The kind that Nan says is spelt with a capital B.

Mum was all quiet on the way home from school yesterday. Miss Horridge, who's my teacher, went up to her in the playground at home time while me and Stan and his best friend Arthur Malik were on the wooden pirate ship, and Miss Horridge was showing Mum the essay. I knew it was my 'When I Grow Up' essay because I was at the top of the mast and I could see the swirly letters spelling Billy Grimshaw on the front that Big Lauren did with her gel pens. And I saw

Mum nod and then put her hand over her forehead like when she has a headache or Stan has wet the bed again, and when she came to get me and Stan her eyes were shiny and wet. And all I could think while we walked up Brunel Street was that I should have said I wanted to be a footballer, like Stephen Warren and Kyle Perry did. Or Leona Lewis, like Big Lauren next door. I told her she can't actually be Leona Lewis because she's not even a bit black, she's ginger, and also Leona Lewis is Leona Lewis, but Big Lauren said she can be anything she wants to be. She read it in a magazine.

When we got home, Mum told Stan to play outside on his scooter and made me sit at the table. And then she said the same stuff as before, that Dad isn't a spy he's a reporter. And that he's not coming to get me to take me to work in MI5 or anywhere else for that matter so I might as well forget about it.

But she's still 'in the dark' about his real job, so it's not her fault.

But that wasn't the capital B bit. We found out in

Doctor Who. Mum actually turned it off to tell us. Even her boyfriend Dave was a bit annoyed because he was watching too. It's his third favourite programme after *Battlestar Galactica* and *Stargate SG-1*. Anyway, everything was excellent up until then because the Doctor had just sealed the pilot inside his suit to stop the meat-eating Vashta Nerada devouring him alive, and Stan was scared and felt sick so I got to eat his half of a Milky Way Ice Cream. But then Mum came in and switched it off just as the creatures got inside and started eating him and said she had something to tell us both. Dave said, 'Now's not a good time, Jeanie.' And I thought he meant because of the Vashta Nerada, but Mum just said, 'It's never a good time, Dave.' And then I knew it wasn't about *Doctor Who* at all. Because Dave got out of the green chair and put his arm around Mum. And I got that funny feeling in my stomach and my legs when they get sort of electricity inside them, and I tried to concentrate on something else like Dr Singh, who's our doctor and who has really big hands, said to do. So I concentrated on Dave's arm and stared at it really hard to make it move by the power of my mind (which is called telekinesis, I saw Derren Brown do it on telly). But it didn't work. Instead the arm squeezed around Mum's waist and her face went a bit red and she said, 'We've got some very exciting news and – Stan put that remote down please' because Stan was trying to turn the telly back on to see if the pilot was eaten completely. 'The thing is, we're going to get MARRIED, isn't that amazing?'

And then everything went totally quiet. And the word MARRIED sort of shone madly and hung there in the air like it was an actual thing and you could touch it. And I could see it all red and hot and alive in front of me. And it was like all the excellentness had been sucked out of the room by that word MARRIED, like it was a Death Eater or a Vashta Nerada. And I didn't want to be in the room any more with a Death Eater so I just ran.

Mum didn't come upstairs straight away. I heard Dave say, 'Leave him, Jeanie. Let him calm down.' But I didn't calm down. I got out my logbook.

A logbook is kind of like a diary, but for more important things than dentist appointments or which celebrities you fancy, which is what Big Lauren puts in hers. Tip Number 7 in the *Zac Black Annual* is *Don't trust anyone* and Tip Number 8 is *Put it on paper*, i.e. you should write down the things that happen all around you, even stuff that doesn't seem unusual at the time, because, according to Zac, villains *DO NOT go round twirling moustaches like in cartoons, they're all around us, disguised as ordinary people, doing ordinary jobs.* Like his mortal enemy Dr Van Fleet, who's a doctor. And Vespa Morris, who's a nurse. Like Dave. So I'm keeping a record of everything Dave does, just in case. Like the time he took Mum away for a night to Wales and didn't take me and Stan even though we begged him to because they were going to the beach. And like when he shouted at Stan for spilling Fruit Shoot on his mobile phone so that the keys stuck and he couldn't do any phoning for a day until his friend Dave Two, who's also a nurse but has a tattoo of Daffy Duck on his arm and comes from Bolton, lent him his old Nokia.

And like him saying, 'Leave him, Jeanie.'

After I'd written it down, I hid the logbook again up the chimney bit in the fireplace in my bedroom. But I still felt weird, so I had to lie down on my bed and count my glo-stars on the ceiling, just to make sure there were still fifty of them. (There were fifty-three once but Stan climbed on the wardrobe and picked part of Orion off.) But, when I got to twenty-seven, I could hear the door opening, then I felt Mum sit down next to me on the blue duvet. But she didn't say anything, she waited for me to get to fifty, because otherwise I'd have to start again from one. Then she stroked my hair until the electricity feeling stopped, like Dr Singh told her to.

'It's going to be fine, Billy,' she said. 'You'll see. It'll be fun. Just a big party, like at Nan's birthday.' But Nan's was just for her seventy-fifth. Nan didn't say, 'I do' and wear a big white dress. She wore blue trousers and a cardigan. And Nan didn't have to go home with Dave until death do them part.

Mum said, 'Nothing will change.' But she's wrong. Everything will change. It already has. It was OK when Dave lived on Pilkington Street. Then we only saw him when he came to pick Mum up, and Nan babysat for us and she let us eat Sugar Puffs for tea and stay up until the news at ten. But now he's here all the time, in Dad's black chair, and he eats all the Sugar Puffs and kisses Mum with tongues, which is gross, and she could catch glandular fever or MRSA off him. Big Lauren says she has seen an MRSA once, it was green and the size of a Rolo. But she also says she has met a vampire, which I know for a fact is a total lie. Anyway, the point is, he will never not be here now. Every time I come home from the park or from school, he'll be here. Just sitting in Dad's black chair. And if Dave's in the black chair, it means Dad can't come home.

So now I know who my mortal enemy is. It's Dave.

Sunday
1st June

Stan is totally happy about the wedding. At breakfast he asked if he could call Dave 'Dad' once they're married. Mum said we could call him what we like and I said, 'Mental Dave' and she said no. Then Mum asked us if we wanted to be double-barrelled, i.e. Billy and Stan Grimshaw-Jones. I said not likely. Stan said yes. It's because he thinks it will make him more like Jake Palmer-Thomas who's second toughest in Year 1. Also he likes Dave because Dave gave him a Millennium Falcon off eBay, only one of the cargo jaws fell off last

Thursday. I said he should ask our dad for a better one for his birthday but Stan said Dad didn't even send him a card until two days late last year. I said it was because he was on an undercover mission in the field but Mum did that thing where she rolls her eyes, and said it's because he's got his priorities wrong.

Then I asked Mum when the wedding is and she said five weeks, yesterday. Which is only thirty-four days. So I said, 'Are you pregnant?' Because Big Lauren's mum Paula, who works in the betting shop on Whitehawk Road, got married to Alan and three months later Lauren got a baby brother called Jordan. Mum laughed then and a cornflake flew out and stuck on the Great British Buildings calendar. She said she wasn't pregnant but that they didn't want to wait around because 'when you know, you just know'. I said, 'Know what?' She said, 'You'll find out one day.' Which is what she always says when she thinks I'm not old enough.

Nan came over for lunch and Mum told her about

the wedding and then about not being pregnant, because that's what Nan thought too because Mum has put weight on. But Mum says it's just back to normal after the divorce, not actual fat (like Big Lauren, who is supposed to lose two stone and is on a special diet, i.e. no McDonalds).

Nan said, 'Well, congratulations, Jeanie. That's lovely.' But I could tell she didn't think it was lovely at all, because when she's annoyed she clacks her false teeth in her mouth when she's thinking and they were clacking the whole way through pudding. Sometimes you think they'll actually fall out, but they never do. Anyway, today they were clacking because she doesn't like Dave because a) he's a nurse and b) he supports Rovers not City and Grandpa Stokes was a City man and c) he's not Dad. Even though Mum says Dad left her, and it's totally Nan's fault that Mum even met Dave. It was because Nan was in hospital to have part of her cut out because of the cancer in it and Dave was supposed to be doing her bed bath. But Nan said no man was coming near her women's bits and Mum had to do it instead and that's how they met and he asked her out afterwards and they went to Slice O'Heaven Pizza Parlour on Mason Road and she had a Pepperoni Dream and he had Vegetable Feast because he doesn't eat meat or fish, or snails because he says snails are living creatures as well. But he's happy to put salt out to kill the slugs in the back garden, which is called hypocritical.

Nan says she doesn't trust Dave. She says he's after her money. Nan has one hundred and seventy-nine pounds in pound coins in three coffee jars in the larder plus more than five thousand pounds in the Post Office from when Grandpa Stokes died. She thinks that once Dave is married to Mum he's going to use his nurse skills to overdose her with morphine. She said she saw it on *Murder She Wrote* once. It was actually for nearly a million dollars then, but Nan says money is money. Mum doesn't know that Nan doesn't like Dave. Nan made me swear not to tell, so I haven't. I'm excellent at keeping secrets. Like I still haven't told anyone about the time Big Lauren accidentally killed the school guinea pig by giving it chewing gum. Then Nan said, 'There'll be tears before bedtime anyway, mark my words.'

So I did mark them. I wrote them in the logbook.

Monday
2nd June

I told Big Lauren about the wedding today. I didn't tell her in school because we sit in the desk in front of Kyle Perry, who has shaved hair and one gold earring and a dog called Killer. Kyle already laughs his head off that I'm friends with Big Lauren, even though I said I was only doing it because she gives me free Snickers. But if he heard me tell Lauren my mum's marrying a nurse he'd say stuff like, 'Is your mum a lezzer, Grimshaw?' Or 'Dave's a stupid name for a girl, Grimshaw.' Dave says it's a common misconception that all nurses are women. But I don't think Kyle

Perry knows what a misconception is. Anyway, me and Lauren went to Mr Patel's on Beasley Street, and I bought a packet of Hula Hoops and she bought *Sugar* magazine and a Mars Bar. I said there were two hundred and ninety-four calories in a Mars Bar but she said she lost half a stone at half-term because of getting the runs in Benidorm.

Lauren said Dave must be the ONE. I said, 'What one?' She said it meant true love, like David and Victoria Beckham. I said but how can he be The ONE? He's dead short and a nurse, and reads sci-fi comics, even though he's thirty-seven. Plus he's vegetarian.

Mum says she's thinking of becoming vegetarian too. It's because Dave is brainwashing her like in the episode of Zac Black when Dr Van Fleet captures Zac's assistant Angelica and turns her against Zac and she nearly kills him but at the last minute Zac realises what's happening and uses his special powers to reverse the brainwaves.

Lauren says love is just mental and is something to do with chemistry and I could fall in love with Rosie

Hoon in Mrs Holloway's class who has a hairy back and everyone calls her Wolverine, or even with Lauren, and there would be nothing I could do about it.

So I said what about Bald Graham who's the man Mum met when she went speed dating with her friend Stacey at the Liberal Club and who was an accountant and had no hair on his head, not even eyebrows. Or what about Dad? He was the ONE first. And he's more than six foot tall and eats loads of dead animals. And then Lauren got excited and said it was just like in the film *The Parent Trap*, except without twins, and not in America, where two Lindsay Lohans make their mum and dad fall in love again, and I should tell Dad and then he might drive back down the M4 and declare his love for Mum because he is the ONE after all and Dave's just a pretender.

And then I had a brilliant idea. It was to send Dad a letter in secret code to tell him about the emergency. It had to be in code because if I wrote it in actual words, Dave might intercept it and be able to read it and thwart the plan. But when I got home I couldn't find my book on codebreaking and Mum said she thinks Stan might have spilled Fanta on it and it stuck together and had to go in the recycling. I could feel the electricity starting again but Dave said, 'Is this for school? I know some code from *WarRaiders*' – which is his favourite game on the computer – 'How about I help you?', but I said no thanks. And I wrote that down in the logbook, because knowing code is the sort of thing mortal enemies would do and could be a vital clue. And I had an even better idea anyway. It was invisible ink, which is on the MI5 website. It's not ink at all, it's actually lemon juice, and you dip a paintbrush in it and write your message and then to read it you just hold it up to a lightbulb or a radiator and the words go brown. So I got Mum's Jif Lemon out of the fridge and one of Stan's brushes out of his WHSmith art set and did the letter. It said:

Dear Dad
Mum is marrying Dave STOP Come and stop
it STOP
Love Billy

STOP means full stop and you have to write it out in case the dot is mistaken for just a mark and the sentences don't make sense any more. I didn't have room for anything else because there wasn't much lemon left over after Pancake Day, and also the brush was the big one because the others were clogged up with pink paint which is Stan's favourite.

I didn't need to look up Dad's address because I know it off by heart. It's 65 Chadwick Heights, London SE3 3PR. I didn't write that with invisible ink. Because the postman probably doesn't know about invisible ink and would think it's a blank envelope and put it in the bin. But Dad will know. All spies do. It's like lesson number one at MI5. I posted the letter straight away so it'll get there tomorrow or Wednesday. Mum asked why I needed a stamp and I said it was a competition in the *Broadley Echo* to win a trip to Africa. I crossed my fingers when I said it. But spies are allowed to lie if it's for the Greater Good. That's what Zac Black says.

Tuesday
3rd June

Dad didn't come down the M4 today. But that's because, statistically, the chance of my letter arriving this morning is only 92.4 per cent. It would be better if I had a carrier pigeon or something because they don't stick to train timetables and post rounds but it doesn't matter because there are still thirty-two days to go before the WEDDING.

And it was a good day because Nan picked us up from school and she lets us have the telly on the whole time and sausage sandwiches for tea. When it's Dave, he makes us do our homework straight away and then play outside so we don't become couch potatoes like Big Lauren and have to have special diets, and he only does vegetarian tea because he won't touch meat with his fingers, not even with kitchen gloves on.

Plus Nan's house is excellent for spying. Her chair is right next to the window and she has net curtains that she can see out of but nobody can see in through. She watches through them all day and is always seeing interesting stuff for me to write down. Like she saw Mickey O'Leary, who's Jade-Marie's dad, riding a Barbie bike down the pavement, and Nan reported him to the police because it might be stolen. But it turned out he was testing out the stabilisers for Jade-Marie and that's not illegal. Nan said it should be because if she'd been on the pavement he could have knocked her into next-door's garden. She also saw Denise from the launderette kissing Mr Wrigley (who isn't married to Denise, he is married to Mrs Wrigley) in the front of his red Vauxhall Astra. She reported that too, but that's not illegal either. Nan says society has gone downhill since her day. She has never kissed anyone but Grandpa Stokes, who's dead, and her cat Dolly, who's named after her favourite singer Dolly Parton, even though he's a boy. Dolly has grey hair, a bit like Nan, and eats cornflakes and is always running away. Once he got on the number 12a bus to Yate. He didn't even have a ticket. Nan went mad at the driver when she found out and said why didn't he tell him to get off? But the driver said he looked like he knew where he was going. Dave said Nan should let Dolly go if he's that determined to be free. Nan told me to write that down as it's another sign that Dave is 'no good'. Nan leaves the telly on now to keep Dolly occupied and not thinking about going up Beasley Street to the bus stop.

When we got there, Dolly was watching *Deal or No Deal* on telly. Nan says he likes Noel Edmonds. Stan watched telly with Dolly but I watched out the window. I asked Nan if she had seen anything unusual. She said, 'Jade-Marie has got new trainers and she only got the last pair six months ago so what is she doing with them, that's what I'd like to know. And that man

at number twenty-three is at it again.' (She means
Mr A M Feinstein. I know that's his name, because
once his post got delivered to our house, which is also
number twenty-three, but on Brunel Street. I've got a
whole section on him in my logbook because his
name is foreign and he might be an agent for another
country, disguised as a normal old man.) Anyway, I
said, 'At what?' And she said, 'Peering.' He knocks on
her door and, when she doesn't answer, he peers in
through her net curtains. She thinks he might be a
burglar looking for security weaknesses. He has no
chance. Nan has four locks on the front door and he's
too big to get through Dolly's cat flap. I said I would
note it down and investigate. What I'm going to do is
try to see inside his house, to see if it's his headquarters
or lair. Mortal enemies have lairs. They're usually caves
or dungeons, with tanks of man-eating sharks and
stuff, but Mr A M Feinstein might have disguised his as
a normal house. I'm just waiting for a good time to do
it. Nan says he goes out every Sunday morning for
three hours at quarter past ten, but that's when I am
supposed to be at football practice. Football was Dave's

idea to help me make friends with boys, i.e. not Big Lauren, but I'm rubbish at it and every time I miss the ball Preston Bates in Year 6 says, 'Loser,' and once he kicked my head. He said it was by mistake instead of the football but our football is fluorescent orange.

When we got home Mum and Dave were back and were writing a wedding list. Nan said Mum already has plates and a toaster but Mum said it would be nice to have a fresh start with new things. It's because Dave doesn't like the plates. Not because of the pattern, which is just totally white, but because they're Dad's plates. He chose them in Ikea. Mum wanted ones with clovers on the edge from John Lewis but Dad said plain was best because it was cheaper and if we broke one, like the time I dropped mine on the patio because we were eating barbecued burgers and a wasp landed on my arm, it only cost 99p to replace it. There are only three left now, so Stan has a plastic *Power Rangers* plate. But they're all going to go to the charity shop with the *Welcome to Bournemouth* teapot, and the chipped blue vase. But not the toaster, because they won't take electrical goods for safety reasons.

They're getting rid of everything for the fresh start. Like, instead of the photo of Dad on Snowdon on the fireplace, there's one of Mum and Dave in Cornwall last year. And I thought maybe they're planning to get rid of me and Stan too, and have new children who'll be vegetarian and shorter than average and want to be nurses instead of spies. And when I thought about that I could feel the electricity again, but then I remembered that it doesn't matter anyway. Because if everything goes to plan then Dad will be here tomorrow. And then it will all be back to normal.

Wednesday 4th June

Dad didn't come. When I got back from school his car (which is a metallic green Volkswagen Golf Mark II F registration) wasn't in the drive and I asked Mum if there had been any phone calls, but she said only the caterers for the wedding, which is actually Mrs Peason from Peason's Bakery, and why did I want to know anyway? I said it was in case the *Broadley Echo* called about the competition. Which is another lie, but I still think it's for the Greater Good. Mum said not to get my hopes up.

She's always telling me not to get my hopes up.

Like at Christmas two years ago when I thought Dad might send me an Alsatian puppy that I could train to be a sniffer dog, and actually it was an *Incredibles* lunchbox with a picture of Dash on it, which Kyle Perry kicked over the infants' climbing frame because he said it was for girls, and the handle fell off.

My hopes are not up now, so Mum will be pleased. It's because I checked on Google and the invisible ink letter is possibly one of the 14.6 million letters that are lost or stolen every year. So now I have to think of another plan. Zac Black says you should always have a Plan B ready in case Plan A doesn't work. I forgot about that.

Thursday 5th June

We're doing a new project at school. It's all about tolerance and respect for other people, even if they're not in the same religion or school, or support Chelsea instead of Rovers, like Stephen Warren (who drank ink because Kyle Perry made him and his sick was blue). Stan's class is doing Islam, which is what Arthur Malik believes in. But our class is doing World War Two. World War Two was last century when Nan was only just born, and was because Hitler, who had a moustache a bit like Mr Baxter who is the school cleaner, didn't like the Jews being in Germany. The

Jews believed in God but they didn't believe in Jesus, and didn't have blond hair like other Germans, so Hitler tried to get rid of them, but England and America and possibly France stopped him.

The best bit is that there were loads and loads of spies in World War Two. They went to Germany disguised as actual Germans with blond hair, and looked for weaknesses and then used them to plot Hitler's downfall. And that is what I'm going to do. I'm going to look for Dave's weaknesses and then use them to PLOT HIS DOWNFALL. Then Mum will see he's totally hopeless and will beg Dad to come back and live here again. So tomorrow I'm going to go and buy a new DOWNFALL notebook from WHSmith after school.

Friday
6th June

Today Miss Horridge let us build an air raid shelter in the hall. An air raid shelter is where people in cities like London and Bristol, which is near here, had to hide when the Germans dropped bombs on their houses. It's lucky there isn't a war now because Dad lives in a loft, which is the top of a building and would be bombed first of all. But probably he wouldn't be there because he'd be in Germany spying anyway. We had to use 'materials around us', because that's what they used in World War Two, so we used the crash mats and two of the dinner tables (which have tops that swing up so they store easily and Kyle Perry swung it once in lunch and everyone's pizza and beans went all over the floor). Then we all got inside in turns, which was brilliant until the table swung down and hit Big Lauren on the head and she had to go to Miss Butterworth, who's the school secretary, and go in the accident book, and Kyle Perry had to go and see Mr Braithwaite who's our headmaster and is called Wing Nuts because his ears stick out like wing nuts, and get told off.

I haven't got a new exercise book though because Mum said we couldn't go into town after school because Arthur Malik was coming to tea and him and Stan didn't want to traipse around the shops, they wanted to play Buckeroo, so I've made a new section in my logbook instead. I've got two whole pages for Weaknesses and a page each for Plan A and Plan B because this time I'm going to be *ready for anything*. They should actually be Plan B and Plan C, because Plan A was the invisible ink, but I decided to start again and pretend I didn't do the invisible ink so that it's neater. I haven't written anything in them yet, because I couldn't actually do any surveillance on Dave because he was on a late shift at the hospital and wasn't going to get back until I was in bed. So instead I wrote down an observation about Mr A M Feinstein, because on the way home I saw him wearing a really long grey coat, even though it is twenty-three degrees outside, according to our school thermometer. Probably he is hiding spy equipment under it. Or burgled things like a DVD player or a computer. Or maybe he's even an alien like in *Zac Black in Space.* Anyway, I've written it down, i.e. *put it on paper.* Because I don't trust anyone.

Not Mr A M Feinstein. And definitely not Dave.

Saturday
7ᵗʰ June

The wedding is in exactly four weeks, i.e. twenty-eight days. It's marked in a big red ring on Mum's Great British Buildings calendar that Nan gave her for Christmas. This month is the Clifton Suspension Bridge, which was built by Isambard Kingdom Brunel which is the street that we live on. Next month, i.e. wedding month, is Salisbury Cathedral which has the tallest church spire in England. It is one hundred and twenty-three metres. Mum says it's a sign. Even though they aren't getting married in a church, they're getting married at Broadley Registry

Office on Park Road, in between the Post Office and Kwiksave.

Dave checked on the internet this morning and statistically it will not rain according to BBC Weather because this hot spell is set to continue until the end of July, which is bad news for gardeners, but good news for weddings. But anyway, it won't be happening in a registry office, rain or no rain, because I'm going to PLOT HIS DOWNFALL. All I need to do is spot his weaknesses and then attack.

I told Big Lauren about the DOWNFALL and the weaknesses. She came round because her mum and Alan were taking Jordan to Zany Zone and she didn't want to go in case she's still concussed from the table. Lauren says her stepdad Alan's weaknesses are Staffordshire Bull Terriers (which people think are pit bulls but they're actually not) and his right ankle, which he broke when he fell off his Yamaha motorbike, and that her weaknesses are Mars Bars and Burger King Whoppers, only without the onion. I said Dave doesn't eat Whoppers because he is a vegetarian. And Lauren said, 'Well that is his weakness then.' Which is true. So I wrote that one down. Then Lauren said she would be an excellent assistant as she has already done one weakness and she's got a digital camera and that we could be a detective agency and spy on philandering husbands, which means ones like Mr Wrigley who kiss people they shouldn't, and make a fortune. I said she'd have to have a disguise though, because she's quite noticeable when she is out because her hair is ginger and long and she normally wears pink flip flops, which make a noise when she walks. She said she would put wellies and her *I've Seen the Lions of Longleat* baseball cap on, which is what Kylie does when she doesn't want to be recognised. Only not a Longleat one. I don't think she has seen those particular lions, she's too busy singing songs in a leotard.

Lauren said we should start tomorrow, and then I remembered about casing Mr A M Feinstein's house in case it's his lair, so I said to meet me at the corner of Beasley Street at ten-fifteen precisely, in her disguise, and to bring her digital camera.

Sunday
8th June

I didn't go to Mr A M Feinstein's house. Dave made me go to football instead. I said I'd walk there on my own, because then I could just go to Beasley Street once I got round the corner and put my disguise on, which is my Rovers hat, but Dave said he had a free morning because his five-a-side is off and his shift doesn't start until half past two, and anyway he wanted to watch. This is a LIE. I know this because I heard him tell Dave Two, who's also on his five-a-side team, that he couldn't come today because he had 'kid stuff' to do, and Donny Death, a.k.a. Donny

37

Walker who works in the morgue, would have to play instead, i.e. he is pretending to be nice and interested in me even though he's actually only interested in Mum.

Then I remembered that Zac Black said you need to *keep your friends close and your enemies closer*, so I thought it was actually quite good because Dave's an enemy and I could use the time to spot another weakness. But all that happened is that he stood about on the sidelines and shouted stuff like, 'Run, Billy' and 'Shoot, Billy, for God's sake, shoot!' And then I tripped over my own foot and got substituted and Preston Bates called me a knob when I walked off the pitch.

On the way home Dave said, 'You're fine, Billy. You just need to keep your eye on the ball more, like Wayne Rooney.' I said, 'I do keep my eye on the ball, just not the football.' He said, 'That sounds mysterious, Billy.' And I said, 'I am mysterious.' And he laughed. But I didn't smile, even though it was a bit funny. Because he might think it's my weakness and use it to win me over and brainwash me into liking him or something. But when we got home I discovered his Weakness Number Two anyway.

It was at lunch, which was shepherd's pie with vegetarian mince, and Dave said, 'Save mine for later, Jeanie. If I don't get going, the Sister of No Mercy' – who is Ward Sister Hawkins who has a moustache even though she is a woman – 'is going to lose it, and I'm already in trouble over last Saturday,' which was when he was late because Stan had put his car keys in the microwave. And then I knew what his Weakness Number Two was. It's the Sister of No Mercy. And now I can do my Plans, once I have thought out all the details, because Zac Black says it's all about details.

I would have done the details after lunch but instead Nan came over and we went to the park so Stan could run about, because if he doesn't do loads of exercise Mum says he's like a caged monkey. Anyway, me and Nan sat on the roundabout while Stan ran around madly with Arthur Malik, and Nan said why was Lauren Hooten standing around on Beasley Street in her wellies and a Longleat cap for two hours. And then I felt a bit sick because I forgot to tell Big Lauren not to wait for me. But I didn't tell Nan that. I said I didn't know. Which is lie number at least THREE. Nan said it looked fishy to her and maybe she's an accomplice for someone, or just mental.

But she isn't. She's my loyal assistant. And I'm going to have to say sorry.

Monday
9th June

I said sorry to Big Lauren at school and gave her my
Curly Wurly, which is only one hundred and
seventeen calories, plus lots of the chocolate falls off
so it's probably even less. But she wasn't that angry
because she saw Stephen Warren's big brother Luke
reverse his car into Mr Wrigley's red Vauxhall Astra
and then drive off without leaving a note, and she's
put it down in her detective agency book, (which is
her Disney Princess notebook that she got for
Christmas from Jordan). Also she got a new hamster
yesterday from Petworld. I asked her if she saw

anything suspicious at Mr A M Feinstein's house and she said no he just went out in a coat, and I said, 'Aha, but why is he wearing a coat in June?' And she said, 'Maybe he's just a cold person, like my Auntie Carla who wears socks in bed.' And I said, 'No, that's the obvious answer, but what about if he's a burglar and is hiding stolen goods or something?' Big Lauren said, 'Maybe the obvious answer is the right answer.' And I thought maybe she's not such a brilliant and loyal assistant after all. But it's not like in Zac Black, where the first Angelica Drew left after ten episodes so she could be in *Star Trek,* and he got a new one, and everyone pretended it was the same person even though they had different hair and one was slightly Chinese. I don't have another Big Lauren. Not even one with different hair or Chinese. So I'll have to make do. So I told her about the Sister of No Mercy weakness and Lauren said she would come over after school to help do the details.

Only when she came over she brought her new hamster with her. He's white and is called Ashley and runs around the front room inside a see-through ball.

But then Stan kicked the ball and Ashley spun too fast and Dave told Stan off. I said, 'You can't tell him off, you're not our dad.' But Mum said, 'No, but he's a grown-up and Stan just kicked a hamster.' I said, 'It was an accident, wasn't it Stan?' and Stan said, 'No, I just wanted to see how fast he would go.' Then Mum said it would be better if Lauren went home with Ashley because all the shouting probably wasn't good for him, and I went upstairs and now I'm too angry to do Plan A and I have to count the glo-stars instead.

There are still fifty. I checked twice.

Tuesday
10th June

We did evacuation with Miss Horridge today. Evacuation was where about 1.5 million children got sent out of the big cities where all the bombs were, and had to live with new families in the countryside and work on farms and stuff. Sometimes they didn't see their mums and dads for four years. And all they were allowed to take was a coat, a comb, a pair of wellies, soap, a toothbrush, plimsolls, sandwiches, raisins and barley sugar. I don't even like barley sugar.

Then I thought that maybe that's what Dave wants

to do. He's always saying our street's too dangerous because all the cars whizz down it to get to Park Road instead of using Mason Road, which has traffic lights and a hump. Maybe he wants to evacuate me and Stan to Nan's house on Beasley Street, which is one-way, so he can be alone with Mum.

Anyway, we got to wear a gas mask which is what all the evacuees had to carry with them all the time to stop them breathing in mustard gas, which wasn't actually mustard but was poison. And when I had the mask on, the smell was like old tyres or Nan's hot water bottle. And I didn't think I could breathe and panicked and couldn't get it off and Miss Horridge had to help me. Kyle Perry said I was a mental case, and Miss Horridge reminded him I am just different. But then he put the mask on and pretended to be a stormtrooper and hit Sean Hawkes with his ruler, and he got sent to Wing Nuts again.

Miss Horridge stopped doing evacuation then and told us that for our project we had to find someone in our family or our street who remembers the war, and ask them all about it. I'm going to do Nan. I'll ask her on Friday when she picks me and Stan up from school. Maybe she was evacuated to a farm, which is why she doesn't like sheep any more. She says they've got the devil's eyes. Plus they're daft, because if one sheep runs somewhere they all follow, even if it's just going to look at a tree.

I still haven't done Plan A. It's because Mum was out with Stacey tonight and Dave let me and Stan watch *Doctor Who Confidential* while we ate our vegetarian cheese on toast. I watched Dave doing the grating and put it under the grill to make sure he didn't add anything extra from the hospital, like warfarin, which is for heart attacks but can also make you bleed to death from the inside out. But it was just Sainsbury's cheddar and Mighty White. When we were watching I had to have my legs on the sofa in case a Vashta Nerada or a Dalek got me. Dave said Daleks wouldn't fit under the sofa and I just needed to stop thinking about them. But it's like when you're on the loo and you think, 'What if a crocodile that lives in the sewer comes up and gets me?' and then you can't get it out of your brain and you have to jump off the toilet really fast. So Dave said I could put my legs on his. So I did, for a bit. But I took them off before Mum got home.

Wednesday
11th June

Today was excellent because a) Miss Horridge told us we are going on a school trip to London. It's to the Imperial War Museum to look at all the things from World War Two.

Also b) we learnt about Enigma, which was a German machine for inventing code, and about all the spies who worked out how to break the code and that's how we won the war. Lauren was pleased because it turns out there were loads of women spies in World War Two who worked on Enigma, and Kate Winslet played one in a film and Lauren says she's like

Kate Winslet, i.e. big-boned, although with Lauren it's not just bones because bones don't wobble unless you have rickets.

And c) I've actually done Plan A. It's:

MAKE DAVE LATE FOR WORK

I did it during tea in my head, when we were eating our Hawaiian pizza (with hardly any pineapple because Stan does not eat pineapple, or the monkey ones in Animal Biscuits even though they taste the same as hippos, and no ham because Dave does not eat pigs, so it was mostly just cheese and tomato pizza really). Mum asked Dave to take us to school tomorrow morning because she has to do an early shift to cover for Stacey who's having her hair done. Dave said can't she get it done another day and Mum said no because the hairdresser Hayley is going to Formentera for two weeks. So Dave said it would be tight because his shift starts at nine on the dot and there's no way he can be late because parking is a total nightmare because of the meters, so he'll have to drop us off on the way, and there had better be no messing.

So that's when I had the idea. I'm going to stop him getting to work on time and then he'll get sacked by the Sister of No Mercy and Mum will tell him to go and live on Pilkington Street again because she can't afford his vegetarian preferences, and they won't get married and he won't poison Nan for her coffee jars and Post Office book.

It's totally the sort of thing Zac Black would do to Dr Van Fleet. Or maybe it is the sort of thing Dr Van Fleet would do to Zac Black. Anyway, it doesn't matter because this time I have a Plan B, i.e. vegetarianism. And I can do the details if Plan A goes wrong. But it won't. Because I know exactly what I'm doing, and it's going to go like clockwork.

Thursday
12th June

When I woke up I was so full of electricity I had to count my glo-stars three times, and then I did some press-ups and jumping, which Dr Singh told Mum was a good way of getting rid of adrenalin, which is the chemical in me that makes the electricity and the sick feeling. Today the adrenalin was because of the PLAN.

At eight o'clock Dave shouted up the stairs and said, 'Get a bend on, Billy boy.' But I was busy getting dressed properly. I put clean pants and socks and my uniform on, which is grey trousers and white shirt and green sweatshirt with St Laurence sewn in yellow on the front, and I brushed my hair a hundred times which is what Big Lauren says you're supposed to do to make it shine, even though hers doesn't really shine, it is more like wiry copper that you get inside telephone cable. And then Dave came upstairs, put the hairbrush away and said, 'Breakfast. Now.'

So I went downstairs for breakfast, which was Cheerios, because it's a school day. But I ate them one O at a time, and chewed each one ten times. Dave said, 'What's up, Billy? Usually you wolf the lot down so quickly you make Jabba the Hut look refined.' And I said, 'I'm just chewing properly like you're supposed to, I saw it on TV.' Then Dave said, 'Well, get a move on, kiddo, because we'll all be late, and I don't want the Sister of No Mercy on my case again.' So I said, 'Well, I don't want to choke, so you'll have to wait.' Then Dave said, 'Are you trying to make me late?' So I said, 'Yes' because it was the truth, and I've already done at least three lies, even though they're for the Greater Good. So he said, 'Right, you've got one minute or there'll be trouble.' And I said, 'What sort of trouble?' And he said, 'Well, you'll have to walk to school on your own because me and Stan are going.' And I said, 'Stan will wait with me.' But Stan already had his coat on and said, 'No I won't, I want to go in the car.' So I said, 'I'll phone Mum at the airport and tell her you abandoned me home alone, like in that film with the burglars and the paint that hits them in the face, which is totally illegal.' And Dave said, 'Be my guest.' So I did ring Mum at the airport. I know the number by heart because Nan makes me dial for her when we're there for tea because her fingers have arthritis and are quite fat and get the wrong buttons and sometimes she rings the Jade Garden Chinese by mistake and they say, 'Take-away or delivery', but she doesn't want either. I didn't get the Jade Garden. I got Mum. She answered in her airport voice and said, 'Jetways, how may I help you?' and I said, 'It's Billy. Dave's trying to choke me to death on my Cheerios and is going to abandon me home alone like in that film, with the burglars and the paint that hits them in the face, which is totally illegal.' Mum went quiet. And I thought she was going to say, 'Run out of the house and go to Nan's where you'll be safe.' Or something like that. But she just said, 'Is Dave there?' And I said, 'He's waiting in the car.' And she said, 'Well, he hasn't abandoned you then, has he, so leave the Cheerios and go to school now and stop being so flaming childish.' So I did.

When Mum picked me and Stan up she was still angry. She said, 'I'm sick and tired of whatever nonsense was going on this morning, Billy Grimshaw. It's high time you grew up and stopped trying to play silly beggars. Dave was helping me out this morning and you're lucky he's there to take you in the car at all. You should be thanking him, not making life difficult for everyone. It's just selfish. That's what it is. Selfish.'

But it's not selfish. It's not just for me. It's for her. And for Stan. And for Nan. For all of us. It's so everything can go back to the way it was before. When we were happy. When Dad was here.

Friday
13th June

Big Lauren says I should've done more detail. She's right. Zac Black would never have let Mum tell him to get in the car and stop messing about. Plan B is going to be miles better. Lauren's going to help me think of it, only we have an actual detective agency job to do first and it is HIGH PRIORITY, i.e. FIND DOLLY.

What happened is that Nan picked me and Stan up after school and when we got back to her house, which took ages because Stan has got a verruca and he says he has to limp or it hurts too much, the telly was on *Deal or No Deal* but Dolly wasn't watching it. He wasn't there at all. Nan said he went out last night at 10.05 precisely and she knows this because it was when the Prime Minister with the huge shiny face came on the news and Dolly doesn't like the Prime Minister, but then he didn't come back in this morning for cornflakes. Nan says she was hoping he would come home for Noel Edmonds. But he didn't.

So I thought of what Zac Black would do, and it was *check out his old haunts*. So we looked in the shed where he sometimes sits on a sack of compost, but he wasn't there. Then we went to Mr Patel's, because Dolly likes Mr Patel because he sometimes gives him jelly worms, even though he's been told a million times not to. Mr Patel says he feels sorry for Dolly because he looks sad, but Nan says that's just the way his face is made. Anyway, he wasn't there. Or at the park, or at the bus stop.

So I said we had to make a MISSING poster with a photo of Dolly and a list of distinguishing features. I am excellent at distinguishing features because in the *Zac Black Annual 1985* it says you should practise observation by doing descriptions of people you know, e.g.

NAN

Hair: Grey and white and wiry.

Eyes: Blue and watery with a black dot on the right one.

(Nan got a bit annoyed when I was looking at her distinguishing eye but I said she would be glad when someone kidnapped her and I knew all about it then.)

Other: Clacky teeth and says blimey a lot.

I asked Nan to think really hard about Dolly's distinguishing features so we could make a list. There was a bit of an argument about whether Dolly was the same colour as smoke or cardboard and how tall he is, but we have agreed on the following:

DOLLY

Hair: Grey.

Expression: Sad.

Height: About an average coffee table.

Nan has given me a photo of Dolly for the poster

as well. It's of him with a pair of sunglasses on, which isn't brilliant as his eyes are disguised, but in most of the others he was either half out of the picture or wearing a pink sequinned coat from when Nan entered him into Broadley Fête pet show.

When we got back Mum was still at work, but Dave said he'd help make the posters. I said no thanks, because I thought he might try to sabotage them because he doesn't like Dolly. But he said I could use his scanner for the photo so in the end I said yes, as long as I got the final say on all the words. He said, 'Of course, Billy.'

And he didn't actually try to sabotage them. He showed me how to do a border so the picture really stands out, and laminated them with his laminator machine so the rain doesn't wash the ink off. Then we laminated some other things too, like a receipt from Sainsbury's and Stan's swimming certificate, just for fun. And it was. Fun, I mean. But then I remembered how Dr Van Fleet is nice to Zac Black, and says he's reformed, but it turns out it's all a pretence and he tries to drown Zac in the Sea of Screaming Eels, so I thought some bad things about him before I went to sleep, just to remind me he's my mortal enemy.

Saturday
14th June

When I woke up I remembered that I'd forgotten to ask Nan about World War Two, because of Dolly going missing, so I asked Mum if I could go round there this morning. Dave said he'd drop me in the Ford Fiesta Zetec but I said I'd go on my own thanks all the same, because it's just a ploy to make Mum think he likes me. Mum said OK, but she's going to pick me up from Nan's at half past eleven because we're all going into town minus Dave. I said, 'What for?' and she said, 'It's a surprise.' But I don't like surprises. The last surprise was her marrying Dave and the one before that was Dad leaving. So I'm not excited at all.

On the way to Nan's I put up Dolly posters with drawing pins and some blu-tack. I put one on our gate, one on the bus shelter and one in Mr Patel's window. Plus there's one in our window and one in Nan's, which is five. I said to Nan we'd find him soon, definitely. But Nan said she didn't think so, because she thinks he's been stolen by Mr A M Feinstein. According to Nan, Mr A M Feinstein went out at twenty-five past eight last night and didn't come back until the bongs went on the news and then he was carrying something big and heavy, i.e. Dolly. She said that's why he's been casing her joint, i.e. he's a catnapper. She says she's been watching her letterbox all morning for a ransom note demanding her coffee jar money. I said Mr A M Feinstein doesn't know about the coffee jar money but she said he could have seen her counting it last Tuesday because one of the nets was in the wash and so her security was compromised. I said I would investigate. I'm going to do it tomorrow instead of football, because Dave's at work and Mum has to take Stan to Arthur Malik's in the morning, so I'm walking to football on my own. Except I won't be. Because I'll be walking to Beasley Street instead.

Then I asked Nan about World War Two. She said she was six when it started and twelve when it finished and mostly it was brilliant because everyone was full of something called Dunkirk spirit, and they sang a lot of songs and her mum knew every single person on her street, not like now where there are two families who never say hello to her, and Mr A M Feinstein who Nan never says hello to. The bad things were that a) Great Grandpa O'Hagan, i.e. Nan's dad, got his leg blown up and couldn't walk for the rest of his life and b) there weren't any sweets because of rationing. Rationing was a bit like where we're only allowed Coco Pops on Sundays, except it was everything on every single day, and instead of Mum checking the packet to see if any are gone, it got marked in a special book at the shop and if you had any secret food in the house then the police might come and confiscate it. Also there were no bananas at all.

Then Nan got a bit teary remembering all the singing and fun, and even more teary because normally when she is sad her and Dolly drink Baileys to cheer themselves up, but now Dolly is gone. But then Mum arrived with Stan and honked the horn to make me come out, otherwise she has to get Stan out and strap him in again because he goes mental if he's left alone in the car. And then Nan stopped looking sad, and said, 'Mr Feinstein did it, mark my words.' So I did. I wrote them down in my schoolbook, where I was writing about the rationing, and went out for the surprise.

The surprise wasn't a good one. It was suits for the wedding. They're blue and shiny and have shirts and stripy ties. Stan wore his home and is watching TV in it. Mum says he has to take it off before tea in case he gets spaghetti hoops down the front because it's dry clean only which costs a fortune. Mum tried on her wedding dress in the shop as well. It's gold and the skirt sticks right out and she said she'll have to shave her legs because she looked like a yeti so we'd have to imagine that bit. Then she said, 'How do I look?' And I said, 'Whatever.' So Mum asked Stan instead and he said like Princess Leia in *Star Wars*. He is obsessed with *Star Wars* mainly because Dave is. But she did look a bit like a princess I suppose. I hope Dave doesn't wear a Jedi outfit to the wedding like he wore to Big Lauren's mum's fancy dress party last year. Although obviously none of us will be wearing anything. Not that we will be in the nuddy. I mean that the wedding will be off. Because of the DOWNFALL.

I am going to do Plan B as soon as I've found Dolly at Mr A M Feinstein's. Big Lauren can't come because she has to go to her cousins in Swansea, so it's a solo mission. But, like Zac Black says, 'That's the way I like it.'

Sunday
15th June

Something else Bad has happened. It's not as bad as the wedding. But it still has a capital B.

Everything was fine at breakfast, even when Mum asked why was I wearing a woolly hat to go to football, wouldn't I be hot? I said it was in case Preston Bates kicked my head again and she just rolled her eyes at Dave, which is code for, 'That boy is odd.' Anyway, then Dave went to work in the Ford Fiesta Zetec and Mum took Stan to Arthur Malik's in the Toyota Corolla and I walked to Beasley Street. But when I got to the end of the road, Kyle Perry was sitting on his front wall, which is actually just some broken concrete because his dad knocked it down with his van by mistake, and he said, 'Oi, Grimshaw, where are you going?' And I said, 'Nowhere.' Then he said, 'What are they?' and he was pointing at my binoculars so I said, 'Binoculars. For seeing things at a distance.' Then Kyle stood up and he is quite a few centimetres taller than me and said, 'Want to come with us?' And I said, 'I can't, I have to go to Beasley Street.' But Kyle said, 'You said you was going nowhere.' Which was true. So in the end I said yes because I couldn't tell him about Mr A M Feinstein and Nan's cat Dolly, because he'd laugh, and I couldn't tell him about football because he knows I am rubbish at football and he'd laugh. So that is how I ended up in Mr Patel's as a decoy.

Kyle said I had a good face for a decoy, because I didn't have an earring or shaved head and I looked like a complete geek, which is good for shopkeepers and also teachers etc., because geeks do not generally steal. So I had to talk to Mr Patel about Dolly the cat still being missing while Kyle took three packets of cola bottles and some strawberry bootlaces and put them inside his jacket. Mr Patel said it was sad because Nan was his best cat food customer as well, and she hadn't bought any for a week and had only been in once for the *Echo* in case there was a headline story about Dolly, which there wasn't. And all the time the electricity in my stomach was going mental and I thought I might actually be sick until I heard the bell on the door ding and I knew Kyle had got away. I said, 'I've got to go.' And Mr Patel said, 'Here, son.' And he held out a Double Decker. I said, 'No, you're all right.' But he said, 'Take it. You're a good boy, Billy.'

But I'm not. I'm not good. Because I haven't found Dolly or cased Mr A M Feinstein or been to football. Instead I've helped Kyle Perry steal from Mr Patel, and I've two bags of Haribo that Kyle gave me as my share of the deal and a Double Decker, which I don't even like, and I can't tell Mum because then she'll know I didn't go to football.

I've put the stuff up the chimney with the logbook. But I still feel sick and there's so much electricity in me that I've done forty-seven press-ups and ten jumps and counted the glo-stars and I'm still tingling. Mum said maybe the football isn't such a good idea because it's got me all over-excited, and maybe she needs to check with Dr Singh and get more tests done, but I said no I am definitely going next week and can Dave take me please in the Ford Fiesta Zetec. And then Mum smiled, because she thinks it's because I like Dave now. But I don't. It's just that I don't want to be a decoy and steal things. I want to be a spy and work for the Greater Good.

Monday
16th June

The Bad thing number two has got worse.

I thought today would be a good day because there was no school because it is an INSET day, i.e. the teachers are doing learning for once (not an INSECT day, which is what Stan thought, i.e. with loads of beetles everywhere). Mum was at work and Dave's friend Dave Two was coming round to play *WarRaiders* on the computer, which usually means me and Stan can do whatever we like, i.e. make an obstacle course in the garden with the mini trampoline and the slide. Anyway we were jumping off the slide on to the trampoline and I heard the doorbell go, because it is really loud and plays 'Clair de Lune'. Then Dave came out and said, 'Your friend's here, Billy.' And at first I thought it was Big Lauren, but then I remembered she was still at her cousins' in Swansea, and I felt a bad feeling in my stomach again, and when I went inside it got worse, because Kyle Perry was sat on the sofa in the front room in a shiny tracksuit and gold necklace with a K on it. Dave said, 'Would you boys like some Coke?' Kyle said yes and I nodded. Then, when Dave went to get it from the kitchen, Kyle said, 'Have you told anyone about yesterday?' And I said no. And he said, 'Well, don't, because I'll be watching you,' and he did the sign that means 'I'm watching you' off that film with Robert de Niro. And I said, 'I won't tell anyone. I swear.' Then he said, 'Mr Patel is a muppet anyway. He smells of curry.' And I said, 'Yeah', even though that's not being tolerant and respectful of people, and is why wars start. As soon as I'd said it I felt the electricity jump inside me again, so that when Dave came in with the Coke and a packet of Jaffa Cakes I knew I wouldn't be able to swallow any down and they'd be stuck in my throat. But Kyle didn't have electricity. He drank all his Coke and ate seven Jaffa Cakes, which is almost as many as Big Lauren. Then he did a burp and said, 'Your dad's all right.' And I said, 'He's not my dad, he's Dave.' So Kyle said, 'Where's your real dad? Is he dead?' and I said, 'No, he lives in London. He's a spy.' And Kyle said, 'For real?' and I said, 'Yes. He lives in a loft and works for MI5.' And Kyle said, 'I wish my dad lived in London. He works down the welders on the ring road.' Then he went a bit quiet like he was thinking about something or maybe he was just looking at the stain on the floor where Stan trod on a chocolate button. Then he looked at me and said, 'Got to go. See you in school, Grimshaw.' And I said, 'Yeah.' And he went.

And Dave said, 'Your friend seems nice, Billy.'

But he's not my friend. And he's not nice. Not at all.

Tuesday
17th June

When I woke up I still felt sick because of the stealing and Kyle Perry being my friend so I told Mum I had stomach-ache, which was true. But Mum said, 'Not today for heaven's sake, Billy, Dave's on a double shift and I can't afford to be off before the wedding.' And she took my temperature with Dave's digital thermometer and it was 36.9 Celsius, which is normal. So I had to go. And all the way in Mum was in a bad mood. It's because she is annoyed with me for being friends with Kyle Perry because he's a bad influence, and annoyed with Dave for letting him in the house and also for not agreeing he is a bad influence. Dave says Kyle's probably misunderstood and has a hard time at home. I said I didn't invite him and it's not my fault if he likes me. But she said, 'Just try to ignore him.'

And I tried to. When I walked into the classroom I sat straight down next to Lauren and pretended not to hear Kyle say, 'All right, Grimshaw?' And when he passed me a cola bottle under the table I just let it roll on to the floor and Big Lauren picked it up and ate it. But at lunch he made me notice him. I was on the field with Big Lauren reading *Heat* magazine but he came over and said, 'Bog off, Fatty,' to her which isn't respectful either, but she did bog off because she's scared of Kyle Perry. Then Kyle said, 'You're my mate now, you don't have to hang around with fat girls any more.' I said, 'She's not fat, she's big-boned.' But Kyle looked at me like I was mental so I said, 'And she's not my friend.' He shrugged and said, 'Whatever. Anyway, you're my lookout, Spy Boy. Come with me.'

And so I did. Because part of me, the boy part, was

scared to say no. And because another part, the spy part, liked being 'Spy Boy'. But I wished I hadn't. I wished I'd listened to Mum and pretended to be deaf or blind or dead or something. Because then he did another bad thing.

He went and found Sean Hawkes, who has diabetes and is called Sugar-Free Sean, and made him go behind the bike shed. And then Kyle took his rucksack off him and got something out. It was a *Mario* computer game and I know it was new because Sean was showing it to Stephen Warren in registration. Then Kyle threw the rucksack back and said, 'Thanks, Sean.' And all the time I was supposed to look out for Wing Nuts or Miss Horridge or Mrs Peacock who is our dinner lady. And I tried to. I tried to look at the field. I tried to make my eyes move but they wouldn't. They just looked at Kyle and what he was doing. And it was like I was doing it too. Holding Sean's head against the wall. Jabbing my fingers in his face. Taking his stuff. Even though I was just standing there, I was still guilty.

Then it was over and Kyle grabbed my arm and

made me run back to the main field. I said, 'But he'll tell.' And Kyle said, 'No he won't. There's two of us and only one of him.'

And I thought that, if I was with Sean, then Kyle would be the one on his own. And I wondered if that would make a difference. But then I thought that maybe Sean would be the one with Kyle, and I would be the one being held against the wall. And I didn't know which was worse.

After school, Big Lauren came over and Mum let her in before I could say no. She came up to my room and sat on the blue duvet and said, 'Why are you hanging out with Kyle Perry? He's a headcase.' I said, 'I'm not, he's hanging out with me.' And she said, 'Yeah, right', which means 'That is a lie.' Then she said did I want to think of Plan B about vegetarianism but I said no thanks. Because I didn't want to do plans. I just wanted to count the glo-stars and make the feeling go away.

Wednesday 18th June

Sean Hawkes has got a bruise on his wrist. It is from where Kyle grabbed it. I know this because he sat next to me at lunch which is where Big Lauren normally sits only she was sitting next to Karen Connolly today who is her second best friend after me. And he said, 'You have to tell Wing Nuts or Miss Horridge what happened,' but I could see Kyle Perry on the free dinners table and he did the sign that means, 'I'm watching you.' So I said, 'What are you talking about?' Sean said, 'Behind the bike shed. I know you were there.' But Kyle was still watching me so I said I needed the toilet and I just got up and went to the loo. And I didn't even come out when Mrs Peacock knocked on the door and said, 'Are you all right in there, Billy Grimshaw?' I said, 'Yes, thanks.' And she went away.

But the sick feeling didn't and at break I said to Miss Horridge I was ill and couldn't go outside so she said, 'OK, get your bag, you had better go and see Miss Butterworth. Someone can go with you.' And I said, 'I'll go on my own,' but Kyle said, 'I'll go, miss,' and Miss Horridge is always trying to get him to be more responsible and caring so she was all happy and said, 'That is very kind, Kyle. Thank you.' But on the way he made me go into the junior toilet and he said, 'Here you go.' It was the *Mario* computer game. The one he stole off Sean. I said no thanks but Kyle said, 'It's yours. Instead of that *WarRaiders* Dave was playing. That's rubbish. Anyway, you're my mate now.'

So I took it. Because I had to. And I pushed it to the bottom of my bag where no one could see it. And then I went to Miss Butterworth and told her I felt sick, and she said, 'Oh not another one,' because there's Norovirus going round at the moment, and that I'd better lie down and she would call my mum. So she called the emergency contact number and said, 'The cavalry's on its way.'

But when the cavalry got here it wasn't Mum, it was Dave. And I started crying. And Dave just picked me up and carried me to the car even though he is short and a nurse and not a secret agent and I stopped crying so much because it felt a bit safe.

When I got home I went upstairs but not to bed. I had to put the game up the chimney with the sweets and the logbook. And I tried to forget about them and just think about feeling safe when Dave was carrying me. But it was like they were all glowing through the wall, like the stars, and shouting, and I could see them and hear them, even when I shut my eyes and put my hands over my ears.

I kept thinking Dave or Mum would hear them as well, but when Mum came up she just stroked my head again. And she said, 'I'm so sorry, Billy. I shouldn't have sent you in. I didn't listen. I'll stay off tomorrow. Stacey can cover.'

And after a while the game and the sweets quietened down. And there were still fifty glo-stars. And then I wasn't scared of Kyle Perry, I was annoyed. Because he was distracting me from the important stuff. Like finding Dolly. And getting rid of Dave. And getting Dad back. And I knew I needed to get my eye back on the ball, like Wayne Rooney.

Or Zac Black.

Thursday
19th June

I did Plan B today. Not just thought of it. But actually did it. It was a surprise, even to me. But Zac Black says it's all about surprise. And details. But mostly surprise.

It was because today was bangers and mash for tea. Mum said it at breakfast, when she was being extra nice to me because of making me go to school yesterday. She said if I felt better by teatime I could have bangers and mash. And then the idea just came into my mind and hovered there all big and shimmering and I knew what I had to do. I had to do the GREAT SAUSAGE SWAP. So after my toast and Lucozade, which is what Mum always gives us when we are ill, I said I had to go back to bed to recover a bit more, but actually it was to do the details. So by the time Dave came back from work I knew exactly what was going to happen.

What I did was, while Mum was tidying Stan's room, which she says is a complete bomb-site because his Playmobil is all over the floor and there's felt tip stains on the duvet, I put some of our normal sausages inside Dave's Linda McCartney vegetarian sausages box and put the real Linda McCartney ones in the bin under a banana skin and some potato peel. So when Mum did tea she cooked just real sausages but in two separate frying pans because Dave doesn't like meat atoms on his food. Mum said, 'It's amazing how realistic those Linda McCartney's are, I don't think I'll miss meat at all if I give it up.' And I thought, 'That's what you think.' At the table Dave poked his sausages and said, 'Are you sure these are Linda's?' and Mum said, 'Of course, what do you think I'm trying to do? Poison you?' And I thought chance would be a fine thing. But Dave cut a piece with his knife and put it on his fork and I watched as he opened his mouth and put it in. And he chewed, and it was like it was in slow motion, because it took ages and all the focus was on his mouth, but eventually he actually swallowed. And cut another piece. And another. Until he had eaten two out of his three sausages. I said, 'Are you enjoying your bangers and mash, Dave?' and Dave said, 'Why thank you, Billy, yes I am. Are you?' And I said, 'Yes, I feel a lot better now.' And Stan said, 'Those aren't Linda's, those are real ones – look, there's some gristle.' And Dave looked at his fork and then he went all pale and then ran to the loo and I heard him spit out the sausage and cough. But no sick came up.

Mum went after him and I heard her say, 'Sorry, Dave. I'm so sorry.' And he said, 'Christ, Jeanie, didn't you check?' And she said, 'They were definitely in the Linda box.' And then it all went quiet. And when Mum came back in her lips were really thin and her forehead was all creased and she said, 'Billy Grimshaw, did you swap the sausages over so that Dave ate meat?' And I said, 'Why doesn't Dave eat meat? It's not normal.' And she said, 'That wasn't an answer.' So I said yes. And she said, 'Go to your room, now. I'll deal with you later.'

So I did. Even though it wasn't part of the plan. In Plan B Dave was supposed to shout at her and Mum would say, 'Well, you're stupid for being a vegetarian,' and then Dave would move back to Pilkington Street and Mum would realise she only loved men who ate meat. Like Dad.

When Mum came up she was still really angry. She said I had to say sorry to her and sorry to Dave, and that was the last time she was falling for my pretend illnesses, and she didn't know what had got into me lately, I was completely out of control, and it was a good job she was marrying Dave because I needed some flaming discipline, and Dave was a good man and what had he ever done to me. And I thought, 'Ask you to marry him.' But I didn't say it. Instead I said sorry. To her and to Dave.

But now I need a Plan C. Zac Black didn't mention a Plan C.

Friday
20th June

I had to go to school today. I tried to say no but Mum and Dave were busy arguing because Stan wanted to take his wedding suit in for show and tell and Dave said, 'Well at least it's interesting.' Because she is always telling Stan to take in something interesting, not just his Millennium Falcon like he normally does. But Mum said, 'Are you stupid? He'll have it covered in Plasticine by first break. There is no way he is taking it. Can't he take your nurse watch?' Which is upside down and is stuck on Dave's shirt. But Dave said, 'You must be joking, he'll swap it for a piece of tat, knowing him.' Because swapping is big in Year 1. Stan has already swapped an Ewok for a lightsaber and the light doesn't even work and Arthur Malik tried to swap his brother Archie for a *Power Rangers* water bottle, but his mum said no.

Mum said, 'So it's OK if he swaps his wedding suit but not your watch.' And Dave said, 'I give up' and went to work. And Mum got even crosser and made Stan get a broken Bionicle for show and tell because she doesn't care if he swaps that, and drove us to school and didn't even say goodbye properly. And I wanted to say, 'Stay, Mum.' But I couldn't. Because you're not allowed to when you are in juniors, you're supposed to be grown-up and just walk on your own into class. So I did. I walked on my own, and I breathed in, because you can't be sick if you have air in your lungs, it's a fact.

But when I got into the classroom Kyle Perry wasn't there and he wasn't there at register either. And Miss Horridge said, 'Why are you holding your breath, Billy Grimshaw? Are you practising for the swimming gala?' And so I let it out and said, 'Where's Kyle, miss?' and she said, 'He's got your tummy bug.' I should have felt bad about lying about the bug but instead I was happy because of Kyle being ill and at home.

But after school things went all bad again. We had to go to Nan's for tea and Dolly was still not back and Nan was very sad and didn't want to play poker and she didn't let Stan make a den in her airing cupboard.

When Mum came to pick us up, she said, 'Have you thought about getting a new one, Mum?' to Nan. And Nan said, 'I'm not like you, Jeanie. I don't just trade my men in for a new model.' And Mum looked all pale and said, 'I did not trade that man in, Mum. He left me. Not the other way around. HE left ME.' And Nan said, 'Yes, but why, Jeanette?'

Mum said, 'Billy, Stan. Come on, we're going.' And we got our bags and I said, 'Thanks for tea.' And Nan said, 'At least someone has manners.' Because Mum didn't say thank you to Nan for having us. She didn't say anything, not then and not in the car. Nobody did. Not even Stan who can't shut up normally.

And now everyone is angry. And it's all because of Dave.

Saturday
21st June

Mum was still angry today, which is three days in a row, which is a new record. So me and Stan had to go out with Dave. He said, 'Your mum needs some peace, she's got a headache.' But when he said it he didn't make eye contact with me, he looked at the pink clock on the kitchen wall, which means it was a LIE. According to Big Lauren, you can tell when someone's lying, there are seven signs:

They don't look at you

They cough

They fidget or touch their face

They go red

They get defensive

They try to change the subject

They try to make you laugh

She got them out of a magazine and they're meant to help you know if your boyfriend is cheating on you, but they work for anything. Like when Nan says 'Have you rung him, Jeanie?' and she means my dad and Mum says 'Yes' but she scratches her neck at the same time and then asks Nan whether she saw the snooker last night.

So I knew Mum didn't have a headache really. She wanted us to do bonding, i.e. she thinks that the more time I spend with Dave the more I'll like him. But she's wrong. It won't work.

Dave took me and Stan to Crazy Golf in the park which is the Wonders of the World, except there are nine of them instead of seven because you have nine holes on a golf course, so they've added the Golden Gate Bridge and the Eiffel Tower, which Nan says are just like the Humber Bridge and Blackpool Tower, but anyway none of them are really wonders, only famous tourist attractions.

But I don't think golf is good for bonding, because when we'd finished Stan was the only one who was happy, and that's because he cheated and carried his ball and walked straight through Stonehenge and just dropped it down the Porcelain Tower of Nanking. And Dave got annoyed because he couldn't get his ball to go up the Blackpool Tower and over the Humber Bridge – it kept falling back down and into the grassy bit, where there's sometimes dog poo, and he said, 'That's not in the rules, you can't just carry balls around.' And I said, 'Why not?' and picked up my ball which was halfway along the Great Wall of China and dropped it down a pyramid which is Hole Number Nine, which meant I'd won. And Dave said, 'What is the bloody point?' And I said, 'You swore.' And he said, 'No . . . I' And I said, 'Liar.' And he looked up at the sky like he was looking for an answer, only there was just clouds and crows. And he said, 'Give me strength.' But the crows didn't give him strength, they just cawed. And I said, 'Can we go home now then?'

When we got back we were all still in a bad mood, even Stan because he wanted to have Magnums at the café but Dave said no because he wanted to get back. And so Mum said she had something to tell me and Stan that might cheer us up, i.e. that Dad is coming next Sunday to take us to see Granny Grimshaw for the day, and how about that.

Dave said, 'Nice one, Jeanie.' And went straight back out the front door and Mum went after him. But I didn't care, because Dad is coming next Sunday. And that is PLAN C.

Sunday 22nd June

I told Big Lauren about Dad. She came over this morning after football to see if I wanted to do detecting but I said no because Mum and Nan are still not speaking and I don't want to annoy Mum by looking for Dolly, and Mr A M Feinstein will be back home by now anyway, and I don't want to case his joint when he's in it, in case it is a lair with a tank of sharks or something. Then Lauren said she's got a new dress for the wedding, only it's a bit tight around the middle so she's not allowed Micro Chips for three weeks, but I can dance with her at the disco afterwards if I like. I said, 'What wedding?' And she said, 'Duh. Your mum's.' And I said they weren't getting married. Lauren said, 'Oh have they had a row? My mum had a row with Alan about the sink last week and they didn't talk for three whole hours.' I said no, it's because Mum has realised that Dave is totally wrong for her. So Lauren said, 'Is that Dave on the drive with your mum?' And it was. They were carrying Sainsbury's bags and kissing. Lauren said, 'It looks like it's all back on again. That's love for you. It's all about the making up. I read about it in a magazine.'

I said it isn't love, she's just under his brainwashing spell and my real dad is coming back next Sunday, and then he'll see her and fall madly in love on the spot, and Dave will go back to Pilkington Street with his *WarRaider* games and his stupid upside down watch. Lauren said, 'Not if she's wearing those trousers, he won't' and I said, 'What?' So Lauren said there's no way my real dad is going to fall for Mum again if she wears her baggy jogging bottoms and no make-up. And I said but Dave doesn't like loads of make-up, he says she is naturally beautiful. But Lauren said according to magazines that's a lie, and he's just trying to make sure she's unattractive to other men, because everyone needs to wear make-up. Even people like Kate Moss, who look like they're not wearing make-up, are actually wearing tonnes of the stuff invisibly. I said if it's invisible then why wear it? But she said that's not the point and men just don't understand. She's right. I don't.

But she's also right that Mum does not look like Princess Leia when she's wearing her old clothes, and so we're going to hatch a plan to make sure she's beautiful next Sunday. Lauren's going to do it. She has loads of make-up from her mum, and tongs that make your hair go curly or straight. Then all the chemicals will work and Mum and Dad will be powerless in the face of true love. That's what Lauren says anyway. She read it in the magazine.

Monday 23rd June

Kyle Perry is back at school.

He came up to me at first break and said, 'Tell your mum you're coming round ours tomorrow after school.' I said, 'Why?' But Kyle said, 'Just do it.'

So I did, because I thought she'd say no because she doesn't like Kyle Perry because of the shaved hair and the bad influence, and then I could tell him that I wasn't allowed, and that would be the end of it. But she said YES because she's on a late and so is Dave, and Stan is going to Arthur Malik's, and her and Nan are still not talking because of the Dolly/Dave row.

But maybe it will be OK. Maybe we will just play *NBA Jam* on the Xbox and drink Coke and eat Monster Munch like I do at Big Lauren's. Maybe we won't do anything Bad at all.

Tuesday
24th June

We didn't drink Coke or eat Monster Munch or play *NBA Jam*. We didn't even go to Kyle's house. We went into town and stole trainers.

It was Kyle's idea to go to Shoe Mania, because in there they have all the shoes out on the racks and you don't have to ask for the other one to try them on. Which is a complete security risk, when you think about it. Kyle said, 'Like any of them?' And I did. The ones with lights in the heels that flash when you walk, like Stephen Warren has got. The ones I've asked Mum for about a million times but she says, 'You've already got trainers and I'm not paying another twenty pounds just so you can look like a spaceman when you walk about,' even though astronauts don't wear trainers, they wear special boots because of the zero gravity.

Kyle said, 'What size are you?' I said, 'I don't know.' So he made me take off my school shoes and look inside, and they were a four. So he took the size four flashing trainers off the shelf and said, 'Try them on.' And I said, 'I haven't got any money.' But Kyle said, 'So?' And then I thought, 'I'm only trying them on. And there's nothing wrong with trying them on.' And I looked around and no one was watching me anyway, because all of Jade-Marie's brothers and sisters were in there playing with the Spider-Man slippers and the man who works there was picking them up off the floor and the other assistant was on her mobile phone saying, 'You won't believe what he did . . . I know. I know,' and looking at her hair in the mirror.

I looked back at the shoes and it was like they were saying, 'Try us on, Billy, you know you want to.' And I really really did. And my school shoes were already off so it was easy. I just slipped them on and did up the Velcro. And it was like in Big Lauren's *Cinderella* film, where she tries on the glass slipper and it fits her perfectly, because the trainers fitted really well, like they were made just for me, and when I walked they flashed in the mirrors and lit up the floor. And Kyle said, 'Keep walking, Billy.' And I looked up and he had my shoes in his hand and was walking backwards towards the door. And I knew what he was going to do. And I knew it was wrong. But the shoes fitted so well and looked so good. And the O'Leary kids were still messing with the Spider-Man slippers and the girl on the phone was still saying 'I know'. And so I just kept walking past the racks of sparkly high heels and flip-flops and out of the doors on to Park Road. And I waited for an alarm to go off, or the man to run after me and grab me by the collar. But nothing happened. We just kept going. And then we were running through the town, and my feet were flying in the trainers and flashing at everyone but no one even looked at us. They just carried on shopping and talking and walking. It was like we were invisible.

At the end of Brunel Street Kyle slowed down and then sat down on his broken concrete wall, and I sat next to him and I could hear my heart thump thumping inside me and my throat and lungs hurt and in my side I had a stitch. But there was no electricity. I had run it all away. And we just sat there in silence.

Kyle said, 'That was amazing, Grimshaw.' And I said, 'Yeah.' And just for a second, right then, I meant it.

But it didn't last.

There was no one in at Kyle's to make us tea so we ate Frosties from the packet and watched cartoons on Sky. Then I said I'd better go as Mum would be back at six and would wonder where I was. And I took off the trainers and held them out to Kyle. He said, 'What are you giving me them for?' I said, 'You're all right. I don't need them.' But Kyle said, 'They're not even my size, I'm a five. You nicked them. They're yours.'

So now they're up the chimney too. And I told

another LIE that we just went to Kyle's house and played football in the garden. And I was trying to eat my fishfingers but the Frosties were churning around inside because all I could think about was the time Dr Van Fleet used gamma rays to turn Zac Black evil and everyone thought Zac had done all the bad things and the police arrested him instead and put him in prison and Angelica Drew had to smuggle antidote into prison so he could tell everyone what really happened.

But Kyle didn't use gamma rays he just told me to do it. And Big Lauren hasn't got an antidote. And no one even knows about the bad stuff. They don't even know I've turned evil.

I wished Dad was here. He'd know what to do. He'd go round to Kyle Perry's house and tell him to leave me alone or else he'd use his spy powers and put him in prison. But Dave's just a nurse. And he's short and vegetarian. No one will listen to him. No one's scared of him.

And then I looked up because Stan was standing on his chair singing about Bob the Builder and Mum was telling him to sit down, and I saw it. On the Great British Buildings calendar, underlined in blue biro. It said, *Sunday: Tom – boys*. And I remembered that he's coming, and that everything will be all right then. I just have to wait until Sunday. And then all the Bad stuff will be over. And I swallowed my fishfinger and asked for pudding.

Wednesday 25th June

When I woke up I was still thinking about Sunday and Dad coming, and I was filled with warm. Not electricity hotness. But a nice soft warm, like my sheepskin gloves, or when Mum lets me get into bed with her when Dave's on an early, and she reads to me. And the sweets and trainers and game weren't shouting, they were still asleep. They were invisible. And I ate two bowls of Cheerios and Mum said, 'You're in a good mood, Billy, maybe Stan could take a leaf out of your book,' because Stan is cross because Dave told him he isn't allowed to stand on his chair ever again because he fell off and banged his head on the table. So when Mum was washing up I whispered to him and said, 'It's all right, Stan, Dad's coming really soon. And then you can stand on everything again.' And I didn't even mind when Stan said, 'Shut up.'

Even when I got to school and saw Kyle Perry kick Sean Hawkes outside the hall, I just felt strong and I ignored him, like Mum said. And I thought, 'Dad is my antidote, and now I'm not bad after all, I'm still Zac Black.' And the warm stayed all through history, when we learned about the land girls who were all the women in England who had to be farmers in the war because the men were too busy fighting. And it was still there at lunch when Big Lauren gave me half her Twix. And it didn't go until PE.

Kyle picked me for football. Mr Baxter made him team captain and he actually picked me for his side. Normally I'm not picked at all. I'm left until last with Sean Hawkes, and Mr Baxter just puts us on a team each. But today I was picked before Sean Hawkes and Stephen Warren, and even Sol Faragher whose uncle is the groundsman at Rovers. And I should've been really happy and the warm should've been hugging me inside because being picked is brilliant. But when I walked past Kyle to stand at the back of the line, he winked at me. And the warm evaporated. And even though the sun was shining hard on my head and the playground was shimmering in the haze, I was cold.

And I knew it wasn't over.

Thursday
26th June

Mum and Nan have made up. Mum says it's because life's too short, and Nan is her own mother after all. Nan says it's because Mum needed her to pick me and Stan up after school and Dave was on a double and so she'd run out of options. I said I didn't care, I was just glad no one was mortal enemies any more. But Nan says just because she's speaking to Mum doesn't mean she's in favour of Dave. I said she doesn't have to worry about that any more, because Dad's coming on Sunday and me and Big Lauren had a plan to make Mum impossible to resist. Nan said, 'There's no talking to Jeanie.' But I said love's about chemistry and Dad is the ONE. Nan said she never had any chemicals with Grandpa Stokes, she just thought he had a nice haircut and his trousers fitted properly.

Then Nan made tea, which was supposed to be macaroni cheese but Nan had defrosted cauliflower cheese by mistake and Stan refused to eat it and so we ended up having Sugar Puffs. Nan says her eyes are on the blink. Which is sort of a joke if you think about it. Except I don't think Nan meant it to be funny. I said she could get a seeing-eye dog if she's going blind, or even a monkey. I've seen them on TV. They have them in America and they can stack magazines and even make scrambled eggs. But maybe not a bacon sandwich because of the spreading butter and cutting. But Nan said she doesn't like scrambled eggs and anyway Dolly wouldn't like a monkey. I said, 'Dolly's not here. He's lost or at Mr A M Feinstein's being catnapped.' But Nan said, 'He'll come back. Mark my words, Billy. He'll come back.'

Like Dad.

Friday 27th June

It's only two days until Dad comes home. He's getting here at ten o'clock and then he's going to take us to Granny Grimshaw's house.

Granny Grimshaw lives in Trowbridge and is sixty-five, i.e. ten years younger than Nan. She lives in a big house that isn't attached to any others like ours, or on top of others like Dad's. She lives on her own because Grandpa Grimshaw is in a nursing home because he doesn't know who anyone is any more. Mum said it was a lucky escape. It's because Granny Grimshaw has loads of rules and moans a lot. Mostly at Mum. Mum says Granny Grimshaw never liked her because Mum didn't go to university and Grandpa Stokes was a gas fitter and wore overalls to work instead of a suit like Grandpa Grimshaw. Mum says it's the only good thing to come out of the divorce, i.e. that she doesn't have to put up with Granny Grimshaw any more. That and Dave.

But he'll be gone in two days. And so will Kyle Perry. He sat next to me in circle time and I tried to ignore him because Miss Horridge was talking about the French Resistance and how they hid spies in their cellars, but he kept nudging me until it hurt so I had to look at him, and he said, 'Wanna come over to mine this weekend?' I said, 'I can't. My dad's coming home. From London.' Kyle said, 'What about the spying?' And I said, 'He'll just do it freelance or else we'll be moving to London with him to live in the loft.' And Kyle said, 'Fierce. I can come and visit.' And then Miss Horridge said, 'Billy Grimshaw and Kyle Perry, do you want to go and see Mr Braithwaite and explain why you're not able to keep quiet for five minutes?' And I said, 'No, miss. Sorry.' But Kyle just shrugged and said, 'Whatever.' So he did get sent to Wing Nuts.

At break Miss Horridge asked me to stay behind because she'd like a word. It was actually words, not just one. She said, 'I think it's wonderful that you're friends with Kyle because he could learn a lot from a boy like you, Billy. But please make sure it's that way around. Don't be brought down, Billy.'

I said, 'I won't, miss.'

And I won't. Because Dad will be here. And he'll stop him.

Saturday
28th June

This time tomorrow Dad will be home. And Dave will be gone, because he'll be powerless in the face of chemistry.

Dave has met Dad once before, and I thought they might get into a fight over Mum then and there and Dave would be left battered in the multicoloured gravel, but they just talked about football and whether Rovers were going to go down. But this time will be different. Because of Plan C, which is MAKE MUM IMPOSSIBLE TO RESIST.

Lauren came over to do a trial run this afternoon

to make sure it all goes like clockwork and the make-up is invisibly brilliant. Also Lauren loves makeovers. They're her favourite kind of TV programme after talent shows. She says they're more exciting than *EastEnders*, even when Bianca came back, and everyone always cries when they have the 'mirror moment' because they are transformed from being totally ugly and old into being beautiful and young. Lauren says if she's not Leona Lewis when she grows up she wants to just do makeovers.

She had to beg Mum to let her do this one though. She said it was for practice for one of her Brownie badges, which is almost true because she is a Brownie, but I don't think make-up is a badge, it's mostly sewing and stuff. Anyway she said Ashley had chewed the nose off her Girl's World and her Mum was out getting Jordan a ball pool, so please please please could Mum be her model.

Mum said, 'Can't you do it on Billy and Stan? Stan loves face paints.' But Lauren said no and anyway it would be good practice for the wedding sitting still and letting someone else do it, because Stacey is going to do Mum's actual make-up and hair on the day because Mum will be nervous with shaking hands. In the end Mum gave in, because Lauren said please twenty-five times and it wore her down.

Lauren had got a pink lipstick off the cover of *Go Girl* magazine, blue and green sparkly eyeshadow and a black felt tip, because she didn't have any eyeliner. When she was putting the eyeliner on, Mum said, 'Is that Crayola?' Lauren shook her head. Because it wasn't, it was from WHSmith so it wasn't a lie really.

When she had finished she said, 'Ta-da!' and held up her *Snow White* mirror for Mum to see. And I thought Mum was about to cry at her mirror moment because she was utterly transformed with her invisibly brilliant make-up. Except the make-up was not invisible at all, it was very visible. And also indelible. Lauren forgot to check the felt tip and it was a permanent marker. Mum tried scrubbing it off with soap but it was still visible. Lauren said, 'It'll wear off, honest.' But Mum didn't say anything. She just looked very annoyed. Then Dave came in with Dave Two from five-a-side practice. Dave said, 'You look like a Goth panda.' And then they started killing themselves laughing. But Mum didn't think it was funny at all. She just said, 'Thanks a lot' and shut herself in the bedroom.

Lauren was disappointed about the mirror moment and that no one cried. But I said it doesn't matter because when you think about it, it was actually brilliant to use the felt tip because Mum's annoyed with Dave again and Dave thinks Mum looks stupid. But Dad won't care because of the chemicals. And also because I've hidden her baggy jogging bottoms in the cupboard under the stairs in a Sainsbury's bag, along with her grey knickers and the sweatshirt with paint on it. So now she'll have to wear a dress or her swimming costume. So she'll still be impossible to resist.

Mum came out of the bedroom for tea. Her eyes were red. So maybe she did cry after all. Or maybe it was the rubbing. She and Dave went into the kitchen and shut the door while me and Stan watched *Doctor Who,* but instead of the Doctor and Amy talking to a Dalek, all I could hear was Mum and Dave.

Like Mum saying, 'How the hell am I supposed to go to work looking like this?' and 'What if it doesn't come off for the wedding?' And Dave saying, 'Calm down' a lot. But she didn't calm down, so I concentrated through the door and sent her positive thoughts like Derren Brown. I said, 'Don't worry. Dad is coming and everything's going to be all right, and you don't have to get married or even go to work because Dad must earn a fortune as a spy.'

And then it all went quiet in the kitchen. And all I could hear was a Dalek saying, 'Exterminate! Exterminate!' And then Mum laughing.

And I smiled. Because she'd heard me. And she knew everything was going to be excellent again.

Sunday 29th June

He didn't come. Dad, I mean. He didn't come home at all.

I was eating Coco Pops because it was a Sunday and Mum was looking for her baggy jogging bottoms with her felt tip eyes still painted on and Dave was saying, 'When did you last have them?' And Mum said, 'If I knew that, I'd be able to find them.' Dave rolled his eyes and went into the hall but then Mum's pocket started buzzing and she pulled out her mobile phone and flicked it open and didn't even say hello. She said, 'Don't tell me, something's come up.' And I don't know what the voice said because it was too tinny and high, like alien interference, but I knew it wasn't good news, because then Mum said, 'Jesus, Tom. This is the last time. It's not fair on them or me. I'm the one who has to pick up the flaming pieces.' And then I knew it was him. And I got up and reached to try to get the phone off her so I could speak to him, but she clicked it shut and my arm knocked my Coco Pops and a chocolate river gushed across the table and started dripping over the edge on to Stan's lap and he started crying because he doesn't like to be messy. And all the time Mum just stood there looking at me, but not looking at me. Like her felt tip eyes could see through me with x-ray vision and she was really staring at the wall or outside it or something. Then Dave came in with the Sainsbury's bag in his hand and he saw the chocolate river and Stan crying and Mum just staring with her black eyes and he said, 'What the . . .' And Mum blinked and then it's like her superpower disappeared and she could just see the room again and the mess and she said, 'He's not coming. Something came up.'

I could feel the electricity seeping into me so I dug my nails into my hands to try to make it go so I could be calm. I said, 'It's not his fault. It's work. He must have a mission to do.' And Mum looked at me all funny, like she looked at us when our rabbit Elvis died. And I said, 'Well he does.' And she said, 'Welcome to the real world, Billy.' I said I was in the real world, I wasn't living in the thirteenth dimension or anything, like on Stan's cartoons. And then Mum saw the Sainsbury's bag in Dave's hand and the jogging bottoms sticking out. She said, 'Where did you find them?' He said, 'Under the stairs. What the hell did you put them there for?' Mum said, 'I didn't.' And then she looked at me. And I could tell she knew everything. And her face wasn't sad any more, it was all tight with anger and she shouted, 'When are you going to get it, Billy? He's not coming back. He's NOT COMING BACK.'

And I could feel wetness on my cheeks and my nails digging down into the skin and hear Stan still crying about the Coco Pops and the noise and I said, 'But he's the ONE. He's the ONE.' And Mum screamed, 'No he's not! He never was.' And then the electricity surged like a lightning bolt in my blood and I ran. Not upstairs but out. Down Brunel Street, past Kyle's broken concrete wall, past the cars and houses and on and on until I could hear blood swooshing in my ears and feel my lungs bursting in my chest and my legs buckling underneath me and I knew my electricity had run out and everything went dark.

When I opened my eyes I could see the sky through yellow bars and it was turning slowly like the world in my solar system model. And then a blur appeared in front of the sun and I could hear a voice saying, 'Are you dead, Billy Grimshaw?' And I thought maybe I was in heaven or something and it was God or an angel. But when I sat up there were no angels or pearly gates. I was on the roundabout in the park and Kyle Perry was sitting on the bar with his legs dangling down and one foot trailing on the ground.

'No,' I said. He nodded. Then he said, 'I thought you was busy today with your old man.' And I remembered the phone call and Mum shouting and my body flooded with electricity again.

I said, 'Something came up. He got called out on an emergency. Terrorists on the tube.' Kyle said, 'Muslims, innit.' I said, 'Yeah.' And it didn't feel bad. Not even when I thought about Arthur Malik. Or Mr Patel. Or even Dr Singh, who's always trying to help me with the being different. It felt like nothing. It was like I was so full of electricity, of anger and hate, that there was no room for anything else. Kyle said, 'Come on, Spy Boy. Let's do something.' And right then I knew where I wanted to go. And I didn't care who saw me. Or what happened. I just wanted to get something right. Get someone to come back home. So we went to fetch Dolly.

We couldn't go round the front down Beasley Street, because I knew Nan would be there looking through her one-way nets at number twenty-three, so we went down the back alley, jumping over the broken bottles and dog poo and old Coke cans until we got to Mr A M Feinstein's.

His gate had the number stuck to it in aluminium letters and a hole in the wood where a knot had fallen out. Kyle said, 'Give us a look' and put his eye up to the gap. 'Can't see no one.' I said, 'He's out.' Because it was half past ten – I checked on my watch, which is set according to the BBC website clock, which is accurate to half a second, and I knew he'd already be halfway to wherever by now.

Kyle said, 'Give us a bunk-up.' But I remembered what Zac Black said which was *never take the hard way when the easy way is staring you in the face.* What was staring me in the face was the latch so I clicked it and the gate opened like the wardrobe to Narnia, except on the other side wasn't snow or Aslan the lion or even Dolly. It was just a backyard with a dustbin and a washing line that goes around in a hole in the ground and a house that looked old and empty.

Through the kitchen window I could see a china cup with roses round the rim upside down on the draining board and an old record player like Dad had, but no CD player or DVD or anything like that, which a burglar would have. But I thought it could be a cover. It could all be hidden in the basement with Dolly in a cage with wires on her head and a panel of levers and buttons. And then above the cup, on the wall in a wooden frame I saw a piece of paper. It was yellow and ripped and on it were black inky letters, but none of them were in the right order for English. They said, *Ich liebe dich*. And I felt a buzz because it was code and I was trying to crack the code in my head when Kyle said, 'No alarm.' I looked up and he was right because on the wall was drainpipes and telephone cable but no white box with a flashing red light like at Granny Grimshaw's.

Then Kyle tried the easy route staring him in the face, which was the back door. But this time it was locked, and the windows were shut. To stop Dolly escaping, I thought. And I thought about how Zac Black had broken into Dr Van Fleet's lair, and I knew the only way in was through the glass and we had to smash it and I could feel the electricity fizzing in my arm like it wasn't mine, it belonged to someone else, and I watched the arm reach down and pick up a concrete tortoise. 'What're you doing, Spy Boy?' said

Kyle. But I didn't answer because it wasn't really me doing it, it was the electricity arm and it pulled back behind me and then rushed forward and the fingers let go of the concrete and it flew at the glass and there was this crack and tinkle like when I dropped the plate on the patio only a hundred times louder, and then there was nothing any more in between us just a big hole in the wood with a jagged edge and the smell of cooking seeping through. And then I saw him. Mr A M Feinstein. He wasn't out. He was standing in the hallway through the jagged hole, staring at me with his mouth open like a big black hole. Kyle saw him too and he said, 'Run!' and I felt his elbow knock against my arm and heard the gate bang against the fence and his footsteps disappearing down the alley.

But it was like Mr Feinstein had Derren Brown superpowers and out of his mouth special telekinetic rays were fixing me to the spot because my feet wouldn't move, even when my brain told them to. They were stuck with glue to the step. And then he spoke and his accent was weird, like Dr Van Fleet, and he said, 'Who is it?' And then I realised he didn't have his glasses on. I was just a blur. And the glue sucked back into the ground and my feet heard my brain and ran.

When I got home everyone was in the kitchen. Even Nan. I could see her at the table through the back door and her eyes were wet and so were Mum's and I knew that Nan had seen through her nets and through Mr A M Feinstein's house and saw that the blur with the concrete tortoise was me. And I was scared to turn the handle and wanted to go back to hide somewhere where no one could find me, not Mum and Dave, not Kyle Perry, not Mr A M Feinstein. But it was too late because Stan saw me and his mouth moved and even though I couldn't hear I knew it said, 'Billy'. And Mum and Dave and Nan looked up and the door opened and the shouting started.

Dave said, 'Where the hell have you been? We've been worried sick, I've been driving round the whole bloody town looking for you.' And Stan said, 'You swore! Mum, he swore.' And I waited for Nan to say it was me but she didn't, instead Mum said something. It was, 'Dolly is dead.'

And then it all went quiet and I could see the box on the table. It said, *Walkers Crisps Prawn Cocktail Flavour* on the side but I knew there weren't crisps inside, there was Dolly dead and broken and covered in blood. And everyone was looking at me to say something but words wouldn't come out of my mouth. Not anything. Because I was thinking about what Mr A M Feinstein had done. He'd seen me and killed Dolly as an act of revenge, like when Dr Van Fleet kills Zac Black's dog. And I wondered how he'd done it. Maybe he'd strangled him. Or cut his head off. Or pulled it like a chicken until it snapped. And all the dead Dollies were in my head miaowing and eating cornflakes and watching *Deal or No Deal* and I wanted them to shut up and get out and it all to stop. So I ran up the stairs and pulled the curtains and lay on my back in the dark counting and counting and counting.

I felt her sit down next to me, but she didn't stroke my hair this time, she just sat very still for ages. And I just kept looking at the ceiling at the Plough and Ursa Major and the half Orion. Then she said, 'Where did you go?' And I wanted to tell her, so she could make it go away and make it all right again, but she doesn't have superpowers, so I said, 'Nowhere. To the park.' Then she said, 'I'm sorry, Billy.' And her voice was quiet and sad and I could feel the tears bursting out of my eyes and she picked me up and held me against her and I could smell Persil and lipstick and soap. And I should've felt safe and happy but I didn't. Because Dad was never coming back.

Monday
30th June

Dolly's still here. He's buried in the Walkers Prawn Cocktail crisp box behind the compost heap. Stan said Nan didn't want him at her house in case she got too sad, so Dave said he could stay at ours and dug a hole in the ground with Stan's yellow spade. But it's worse because even if Nan doesn't know about the concrete tortoise and the revenge, Dolly does, and now he'll be waiting to come out of the ground like a zombie cat and attack me at night for getting him killed.

I've moved places at breakfast so I can't see out of

the window and Dolly can't see me. Mum said, 'Billy, will you keep still! You're spilling milk all over the table and I haven't got time, I've got to be at the Registry Office to sort some things before half nine and Stacey can only cover me until eleven.' But I wanted to sit in Stan's chair because he can only see the fridge and the Great British Buildings calendar, so I carried on moving anyway. Dave said, 'I'll get it, Jeanie, calm down.' Mum said, 'I am calm.' But she wasn't. It was a LIE.

When I got to school, Kyle was waiting for me by the wooden pirate ship and I could see his gold earring glinting in the sun like Jack Sparrow – Jack Sparrow doesn't have a shaved head, he has dreadlocks. I carried on walking but he followed me and kept talking saying, 'Are you all right, Grimshaw? You were mad on Sunday. Did he catch you? What did your mum say?' And I could see Big Lauren watching me from the steps with Karen Connolly, and I wanted to go over there where it was safe and talk about makeovers and Leona Lewis. But Lauren didn't smile or wave, she just stared, and I knew she was angry at me for being with Kyle and that now he was my only friend. And Kyle said, 'Meet me at HQ at lunch.' I said, 'What HQ?' He said, 'Duh, our HQ behind the bike shed.' And I thought I didn't have anything else to do or anyone else to be with any more so I said, 'OK.'

But I wish I hadn't. Because that's when he told me the plan. He's going to make Sugar-Free Sean pay us money every day starting tomorrow. Sean has to meet Kyle in the toilets in first break and give him two pounds. And I'm lookout because of my decoy face and binoculars. Kyle says I don't actually do any of the bad stuff, I'm just the sidekick.

But it doesn't feel like that.

Tuesday
1st July

Sean only had one pound fifty and it was his dinner money and he said if he didn't eat his blood sugar got low and he might die, which is true, it happened once in PE. Only he didn't die, he fainted, and had to go to Wing Nuts' office and have an injection. Kyle said, 'Tough' and then he pushed him against the hand dryer which went off and blasted Sean's hair and was really hot and was hurting him, but Kyle held him there a bit longer and said, 'Bring it all tomorrow or else.' Sean didn't ask 'Or else what?' but I knew it wouldn't be good, and so did Sean. And all the time I stayed at the door and looked out for Wing Nuts and Miss Horridge. And when Stephen Warren asked to come in the toilet I said no and he had to go to the infants' where the toilets are really low down and your knees stick up in the air.

But even though I was at the door I saw everything. I knew what was happening. And I knew Sean was crying. But I didn't say anything. Because it wasn't me who did the pushing or the taking. And I thought, anyway, Sean got a free lunch because he said he lost the money on the way to school. And I thought that meant it was all OK.

But it wasn't.

Kyle gave me 50p. I said no but he said it was my share and I had to take it. I put it in my pocket but it shone hot like the computer game and the trainers, and I didn't want to keep it in there so I went and put it in Miss Horridge's collection box for children in Africa, which was our project last term. She said, 'Thank you Billy, you're a good boy.'

But I'm not. Because then she told us about the Holocaust and what happened to the Jewish people, that they got sent away for being different and killed in camps. And even though the Germans who weren't Nazis knew it was wrong, they didn't say anything, so they were just as bad as the killers. And I knew then that I was like a German who saw the Jews go away and said nothing.

But I still kept my mouth shut. Because I was scared. And I didn't say a word. Not even when Sean Hawkes was dead.

Wednesday
2nd July

It wasn't all my fault. Sean brought sandwiches. He should have brought the money, but his mum didn't have any in her purse, so he had packed lunch. And that made Kyle really angry because he said, 'What am I going to do with cheese and pickle, you idiot?' and then he pushed him. And I don't think he meant it to happen, but Sean tripped at the same time and fell down, and it was a bit slow motion, like in films, because I saw every detail, like the exact bit of his forehead that hit the edge of the toilet, and the sound of the crack, and the way his head thudded against the floor then came up again a centimetre and then hit it again, and the blood that came out of his eyebrow and ran down his face. And I heard Kyle say, 'Come on, Billy,' but I kept looking at Sean who was lying on the toilet floor in the smelly wet, with blood all around his head and I couldn't move. Then I heard the door shut behind me and I knew Kyle had gone.

I said, 'Get up, Sean.' But he didn't get up. And he didn't say anything. And he wasn't even crying any more. He was quiet. And the only noise was my heart thudding madly inside me. And just for a second it was like time had stopped for us and then I thought about *Doctor Who* and I wished I could go back in time and I closed my eyes and thought really hard about the second before we opened the door. But I didn't have a Tardis or even a sonic screwdriver, and when I opened my eyes Sean was still there and the blood was making a pattern on the lino and then the door swung open behind me and I heard Sol Faragher say, 'Oh my God, sir, Sean Hawkes is dead, sir!' and Wing Nuts must have come in because I heard him say, 'What on earth happened, Billy

Grimshaw?' And then time moved really quickly and I looked at Wing Nuts and I wanted to say the truth, but what came out was, 'He fainted, sir.' And Wing Nuts said, 'Go to the office and get Miss Butterworth to bring his insulin and call an ambulance.' And I must have stood still too long because then Wing Nuts said, 'Are you deaf, Billy? Get going.' So I did and Miss Butterworth called 999 and got the insulin kit out of her drawer and went back to the toilet where the whole school was waiting to see what had happened. But Wing Nuts wouldn't let anyone in. Not even me. We had to go back to our classrooms and wait. Big Lauren said, 'Is he all right? My cousin in Swansea hit his head on a lamppost and now he's in special school.'

I looked at Kyle but he just kept his eyes on the floor like he couldn't see me.

Miss Horridge came back and everyone started up saying, 'Where's Sean, miss? Is he dead, miss?' She said, 'Sit down, all of you. No, I think he just missed his breakfast and fainted and hit his head.' Then she looked at me and into me and said, 'It was lucky Billy was there. To raise the alarm.'

But when she said it her cheeks were red and she touched her forehead, which meant it was a LIE. And then I knew it wasn't lucky I was there. I didn't save him. He was dead. And even though I didn't do the pushing I still killed him. Because I said nothing. And that is just as bad.

Thursday 3rd July

I had the idea in the middle of the night. I woke up and needed the loo and when I was coming back tiptoeing across the landing I saw Mum standing at her bedroom door in her white nightie like a ghost. The ghost said, 'Are you all right, Billy?' I nodded. The ghost said, 'Go back to bed then, you've a long day tomorrow.' I said, 'Why?' The ghost said, 'Your trip, Billy. The war museum.' I nodded again and the ghost disappeared and it was just dark again and I lay back in bed and looked up. And I stared hard at the glo-stars until they started to move and spell out words and the words said, *Go and live with your dad, Billy*. And I thought the stars were right. Because in London there would be no dead Sean Hawkes and no Kyle Perry and no trainers and Haribo and computer games all hot and loud and shouting and no Mr A M Feinstein and no Dave and no wedding. And that was PLAN D.

When I got downstairs Mum looked at my rucksack and said, 'Crikey, Billy, you're going for one day. You don't need to take the kitchen sink.' I said, 'I haven't got the kitchen sink. I'm just being prepared, like Zac Black.' Dave said, 'You won't be able to carry it.' I said, 'I can, look.' And I did. And I could feel the straps digging into my shoulders and the bag pulling me backwards because inside were all my clothes and my *Zac Black Annual* and books and my Dalek money box for emergencies and the logbook to show that I've been training and am ready to be an assistant. But I just smiled and kept walking. Mum shrugged and said, 'Fine. But don't blame me when they don't let you on to the coach.'

But they did. Mum said, 'Have a nice day. And don't forget it's Dave picking you up. I'm on my hen night.' (Which is where her and Stacey go out with loads of other women in funny outfits and fairy wings like they're at one of Stan's parties.) And I said, 'I'll miss you, Mum.' She said, 'I'm only going to the bingo.' But I didn't mean that and I hugged her tight and in my head I said, 'I love you, I love you.' Mum laughed and said, 'I've got to go, Billy, I'll be late.' So I let go and she kissed me on the forehead and Stephen Warren said, 'Grimshaw's a girl.' So I went up the steps and didn't once look back.

Kyle wasn't on the coach. His mum didn't pay his five pounds so he had to stay behind with the Year 4s and do reading. Nor was Sean Hawkes. Because he was dead.

Big Lauren was there though. But when I got near her seat she put her hand on it and shouted 'Karen, here, I've saved you a place.' So I pretended I didn't want to sit with her anyway and carried on walking down the coach to a seat on my own where

I didn't have to talk to anyone and I could just think my own thoughts.

And that's what I did. I thought about the letter on the bed addressed to Mum, which said sorry, and about Mr Patel and Shoe Mania, and the concrete tortoise and Mr A M Feinstein killing Dolly for revenge, and me killing Sean Hawkes. And I thought about the sweets and computer game and trainers I'd put in a WHSmith bag and left next to the letter so Mum can give them back. And I looked out of the window at Broadley. At the Post Office and Kwiksave and the Registry Office where Mum and Dave would be on Saturday. At the pale brick houses in rows and rows. I looked at all of it disappearing behind me until there was nothing outside but the motorway and green fields. And I stayed like that just staring and thinking all the way up the M4 until the green turned into brown and red and in the sky were gold domed mosques and skyscrapers and a giant digital clock and a sign that said, *Welcome to Hammersmith*. And then I knew we were in London. And I knew that in there somewhere in the millions of people was Dad. And I felt good.

Getting away was easy. Everyone was in the Holocaust exhibition looking at pictures of thin, scared women, and it was dark in there, and everyone was squashed and pushing. I ducked down and slipped behind the curtain and then I was back in the main hall looking down at the life size bomber plane and the other schools and tourists with cameras and guides, and I thought about Tip Number Ten which is *Look Like You Know What You're Doing*. Because then you blend in and no one suspects you. So I just walked like I knew where I was going, like Dolly did on the bus to Yate. I walked right past the security guards, and past the shop, and I waited to feel a hand on my shoulder and someone saying, 'Where are you off to?' But no one did. Not even when I asked the coat lady for my rucksack that they made me leave behind in case it was a bomb. She just said, 'St Laurence?' And I nodded and took the bag and put it on my back and walked out the doors on to the steps and into the traffic and noise and hot hot sun.

I got a taxi to Dad's. I know that it's cheaper to get the bus or the tube but I had twenty-three pounds sixty-seven in my Dalek money box and also I didn't know which bus to get or where to get it. I just stood next to the road and waved my hands at the black car with the yellow light on top and it stopped and I opened the door and said, 'Chadwick Heights SE3, please,' like I knew where I was going. I could see the driver's eyes in the rearview mirror looking at me and thinking, 'Why is a boy getting into my car when he should be at school, and not getting taxis at all but being collected by his mum?' But I smiled purposefully and sent thoughts to his brain, which were, 'I'm not just a boy, I'm training to be a spy on my way to meet my superior agent, who's also my dad, and we're going to fight crime together and save the world.' And it must have worked because the driver said, 'Right-o' and pulled out into the traffic.

But when we got to Chadwick Heights I thought

it had been a trick. Because it wasn't a glass skyscraper. It was a council block like the one Nan used to live in with Grandpa Stokes, with broken bikes on the balconies and washing hanging out. And I said, 'This isn't it.' The driver said, 'Chadwick Heights, SE3. This is it. And that'll be twenty-one pounds fifty, please.' I said, 'But where's the glass windows from the floor to the ceiling and the pointed roof and the flashing red light on top?' And the driver laughed and said, 'Someone's been having you on, sonny.' And I looked in the mirror and he was watching me, waiting to see if I was purposeful, so I got the money out of the Dalek money box, which was quite hard because a lot of it was two pences and five pences and kept rolling under the seats and the driver didn't seem very happy, so in the end I just pushed the whole piggy bank through the glass window and said, 'There's twenty-three pounds sixty-seven in here. You can keep the change. I don't need money where I am going. I will be earning a fortune.' And then I opened the door and pulled my rucksack out and ran.

The stairs were dark and smelt of wee like the

multi-storey car park at the cinema. But I could hear the driver shouting 'Oi, sonny' and I knew I had to move.

Number sixty-five was on the sixth floor. It had a red door and a window that had metal across the glass, so that everything behind was covered in criss-cross patterns like a prison. And I thought, 'It doesn't look like a loft with a bed in the air and orange juice on a tap in the fridge.' But I didn't know what else to do and the electricity was buzzing so madly in me because I knew I was so close, that he was behind that door. So I rang the bell.

He was shorter than I remembered, and his face was covered in stubble like Homer Simpson, and he wasn't wearing a suit like Zac Black or even a shirt and trousers, he was in a Radiohead T-shirt and boxer shorts. And he didn't arch an eyebrow and say, 'Billy, you're here, about time, now the action will really hot up.' He scratched his pants and said, 'Billy? What the bloody hell are you doing here? Christ! Does your mother know?'

But it was him. And I was home.

Inside wasn't like I had imagined either. The floor was swirly carpet like at Nan's, and the walls were all covered with orange paper with chips of wood in it, and there wasn't one big room with everything in it except the toilet, there was just one small room with a bed and a sofa and a TV, and a little kitchen with yellow cupboards that smelt of curry. I said, 'Is this it?'

But I don't think Dad heard me because he said, 'I'm calling your mum.'

There was no answer from home and her mobile was off because she isn't allowed to make personal calls at work and he didn't know the airport number and I said I didn't either, which is a LIE but it's for the Greater Good. Then Dad said, 'How the hell did you get here?'

So I told him about the coach and the war museum and about being squashed in the Holocaust bit and looking purposeful and the taxi and the money and everything. And I waited for him to say, 'Resourceful, Billy, I like it.' But he said, 'She's going to murder me.' And I thought maybe he meant an evil mortal enemy but then I realised he meant Mum and

I thought, 'Why's he scared of Mum? He is an international spy and she is a check-in person at the airport and has no superpowers or even binoculars.' But I didn't say that. I said, 'I'm hungry.'

Dad said, 'Right' and opened the fridge and inside wasn't orange juice on tap, there was a carton of milk and a jar of jam and a pizza box which Dad got out and said, 'This is all I've got in. I don't usually shop when I'm working nights.' I looked at the pizza and the cheese was all hard and dry and the olives were shrunk like fingers after too long in the bath, but I ate it. Because it was Meat Feast. While I was chewing Dad poured me a glass of milk but I didn't tell him I don't drink milk any more, only on cereal, and I'd rather have Ribena, because he has more important things to remember in his head than milk. Instead I said, 'Where can I sleep?' Dad said, 'Are you tired?' I said, 'Not now, tonight.' And Dad said, 'I'm working nights, Billy.' And I said, 'Well, I can come with you then.' And Dad said, 'I don't think so.' And I said, 'Maybe tomorrow then, when you've told the big cheese.' Dad was quiet for a bit. Then he said, 'How long are you planning to stay, Billy?' And I said, 'Until I'm eighteen and can join MI5 like you, then maybe I can move next door, and we can have a special passageway in between like Zac Black and Angelica Drew, so we can be quick in an emergency.'

Dad said, 'Is that what you think I do, Billy?' I nodded. And he laughed. But it wasn't a happy sound, it was sort of sad and angry, and he said, 'I'm a reporter, Billy. Not even a bloody good one . . . Do you want to know what I do all night?' I nodded again. 'I sit outside politicians' houses in the car. And sometimes I look through their rubbish. I stick my hands in dustbins, in the filth. Like a bloody tramp.' I said, 'For clues?' And he laughed the angry sad laugh again. He said, 'For telephone bills that show they've been cheating on their wives, or their husbands. For drug packets. For receipts. For anything.'

I could feel the electricity in me sort of stop and start to cling together and become heavier and heavier like a giant lump of lead sitting in my stomach, and I said very quietly, 'That's still spying.' But Dad got angrier then, and said, 'No it's not. It's disgusting. It's cheating and betraying people. I'm the lowest of the bloody low. I didn't leave to be Zac flaming Black, I left because I was an idiot.'

Then he stopped shouting and put his forehead on his hand and rested it on the table. And I waited for him to say, 'You've passed the test and that was all a lie and I really am a spy and let's talk business.' But instead the doorbell rang.

Dad said, 'That'll be the police. Jesus, Billy, I just don't need this.'

But it wasn't the police. It was Dave. He said, 'Is he here?' And Dad said, 'He's through there. I didn't know. I swear.' And Dave said, 'I know.' And then he was in front of me and he picked me up out of the chair and hugged me but I didn't want to be hugged, not by him, so I kicked and fought and in the end he let go. And I could feel wet on my cheeks and I said, 'Why did you let him in, Dad? He's the mortal enemy.' And Dad said, 'He's not the enemy, Billy. He's Dave.' And I said, 'But he's marrying Mum even though you're the ONE and he doesn't love me and he'll make me call him Dad and we're not even genetic, he only eats vegetables and I want to stay here with you, Dad, I want to be a spy and go out at night and find international criminals.' And then everyone was quiet and I could feel snot running out of my nose and I didn't have a hanky so I wiped it on my T-shirt and tried to stop the crying sound that was coming out of me but it wouldn't because when I looked at Dad in his pants and his stubbly face standing on the swirly carpet with the orange chipped walls I suddenly saw the truth. And the truth said, 'You were wrong, Billy. You were wrong all along.' The truth said, 'We need to go home.'

It was still afternoon when we left London. Dave had found the letter after Mum had gone to work and he called the museum and spoke to Miss Horridge and called Nan and asked her to pick up Stan from school, then driven straight to Dad's to get me. He said he knew where I'd be, he could see it in his head. Like a superpower. Then he said, 'Why didn't you tell me, Billy?' I said, 'You would've stopped me.' He said, 'Not about running away, about Kyle Perry.' I said,

'What would you have done?' He said, 'Stopped you.'

And I thought maybe he would. Maybe he would have known a way to make it stop. I said, 'Does Mum know?' And Dave said, 'No. I didn't want to spoil her night.' Then he said, 'I didn't think you liked milk, Billy.' I said, 'I don't.' And I felt a smile inside me growing like a seed.

But I didn't let him see it. I turned to the window again and watched London disappear behind us, the skyscrapers and mosques and giant clocks. Everything larger and louder than life. And I closed my eyes and let it wash over me like a giant bath of heat and noise.

When I woke up we weren't at Brunel Street. We were on the ring road heading for Sturford. I said, 'You've missed the turning.' Dave shook his head and said, 'I've got something to show you.' Then I saw the sign. The big white H on the blue square. And I realised where we were going.

The hospital smelt of Dettol and cabbage and sounded like a swimming pool, all hollow and echoey. Dave Two was at the desk in his white uniform with his upside down watch. He said, 'All right, Dave, Billy boy.' I looked up at Dave One, my Dave, and said, 'Are you going to work?' But he didn't answer, he just held my hand and walked past all the beds with the ill and broken people to the end of the ward. When we got to the last curtain he stopped and said, 'In there, Billy.' And I thought it was wrong to just look at people behind curtains who might be ill or dying and didn't even know you but he pulled the curtain back for me.

In bed was Sean Hawkes. And he wasn't dead. He was sat up in bed with a big white bandage on his head like in Stan's medical kit and he was reading a *Batman* comic and eating a banana. I looked back at Dave and he was holding something out to me. The *Mario* game. The one Kyle stole. That I stole. He smiled and said, 'Go on.' And I knew what he wanted me to do. And I wanted to do it as well. Because I could feel the smile growing a little bit more inside me. So I said it. 'I'm sorry.'

Sean said it was all right and he knew it was Kyle who did it. I said, 'No it's not, I should have said no.'

But he said it's hard to say no to Kyle Perry. I said, 'Yeah.' Then he said, 'Anyway I get off school and they took X-rays of my head and everyone brought me comics and stuff.' And then he let me sit on the bed and we made it go up and down and Dave didn't even tell us off even though I know he is always getting annoyed with visitors for doing that normally because the Sister of No Mercy says it's not a theme park it's a hospital.

When it was time to go Sean said, 'See you in school, Grimshaw.' And I nodded and grinned. Because now there were two of us. Me and him. Three with Big Lauren, if she'll be my friend again.

Four with Dave.

Dave put me to bed. The letter and the bag were gone. I said, 'Are you going to tell Mum?' He said, 'Not if you don't want me to.' I shook my head. He said, 'Sorry about your dad.'

And I looked at the glo-stars. At the Plough and Ursa Major and the half Orion. But I didn't count them. Not once. Because I was thinking that, even though Dave wasn't a spy and didn't save the world, he had saved Sean Hawkes.

And even though Mum was at Stacey's and Stan was at Nan's, I felt safe.

Friday
4th July

I didn't kill Dolly either. Nor did Mr A M Feinstein. Mrs Webster from Stonar Street found him in Kwiksave. He was looking at the tinned tomatoes. Anyway, a shop girl saw him as well and screamed, even though he's only a cat, and Dolly ran out of the front door and into the road and a Black Ford Mondeo Y registration ran him over. By the time Mrs Webster got there he was all broken and dead so she got a crisp box from Costcutter and took him back to Nan's on her shopping trolley.

Dave told me at breakfast, which was at ten o'clock

because I slept so late. Normally Stan would wake me up at seven with his singing and his Playmobil but he was still at Nan's and Mum was at Stacey's.

Dave said he'd called in sick for both of us so we didn't have to go to school or to work. Instead we had to go and say sorry.

We started at Shoe Mania. We didn't give the trainers back though, Dave gave them £19.99 instead because I'd run in them and they had mud on and were scuffed and one of the light batteries was dead so only one shoe flashed any more. I felt sick when we walked up to the counter but after I'd said it, said sorry, it felt brilliant and the seed inside me grew a bit more and the man in the shop who'd been picking up the Spider-Man slippers said, 'Blimey that's the first time that's happened, we lose at least five pairs a week you know, normally size five ladies, but the CCTV is on the blink and it's probably someone just doing it for the buzz.' And I remembered the electricity feeling and I wondered if that was the buzz and if so why anyone would want it. Because Dr

Singh says it's something working too hard inside me, it's part of being different. But maybe some people want to be different.

Mr Patel was nice too, because of Nan. He said, 'You're a good boy in your heart, Billy Grimshaw, just stay clear of bad influences, they are everywhere. My Ash is in with a bad lot at college. They drink, they fight, they do who knows what. Some kids just will not listen, but you listen, Billy, you listen to Dave, he knows what's right.' I said, 'Except in *Doctor Who*, he thinks Amy is better than Donna.' And Dave laughed and the seed grew a little bit more.

Dave said we didn't have to talk to Miss Horridge today about Kyle Perry or being a lookout or running away. He said that could wait. But we did have to see someone else. We had to see Mr A M Feinstein. When he said that I felt the seed shrivel, because I thought, 'Even if he didn't kill Dolly, what if he's actually a spy or a mortal enemy and it is his lair?' And that maybe we would go in but never come out again, and Mum and Stan would think we'd been kidnapped or swallowed up by a black hole.

But Dave said no is not an option.

I looked at Nan's house to see if she was watching through the nets so she would know we'd gone into the lair and would raise the alarm. But the curtains were still and I remembered only she can see out and we can't see in, so instead I sent thought rays through Mr Feinstein's letterbox saying, 'Don't answer the door, don't answer the door.' But they didn't work because he did answer.

He didn't look like a mortal enemy. He looked like an old man. He was wearing a brown cardigan and trousers and a white shirt, and he smelt like Nan, of musty cupboards. And when he smiled it wasn't really a villain smile, just a normal smile. But then villains do not go around twirling their moustaches in public so it could still be a clever disguise.

He said, 'Come in.' But not how Mum or Dave or Nan say it. He said it in the Dr Van Fleet voice, and my feet started glueing themselves to the floor again and I couldn't come in, I was stuck on the *Welcome* doormat in the porch. In the end Dave put his hand on my back and pushed. Not like Kyle Perry pushes but just slowly, and it was amazing, my feet unstuck and walked by themselves like Dave's hand was telling them what to do, i.e. walk into the front room and sit down in the flowery chair.

Dave stayed standing, but Mr Feinstein sat down on a matching sofa so that all there was in between us was a wooden coffee table with a newspaper and a plate of biscuits on it. He said, 'I know why you've come.' I said, 'Can you read minds like Derren Brown?' because that would be a good superpower. He laughed a short coughy laugh and said, 'And what is your mind saying now? Let me see. I think it is saying sorry.' I nodded, totally amazed, because that was exactly what my mind was thinking, part of it anyway. It was also thinking, 'Where is the nearest exit?' and 'What are the biscuits for?' But Mr Feinstein shook his head and said, 'I recognised you. You're Mrs Stokes's grandson, aren't you?' Which is Nan, so I nodded again. Then he said, 'It was a wrong thing, a bad thing, but you are here now and that is what matters the most.' Then he pushed the plate of biscuits towards me and said, 'Go on, have one.' And I was looking at the Jammie Dodger thinking I would really like it because Mum doesn't get that kind, she only gets Jaffa Cakes and Bourbons, but what if they're poisoned with warfarin, because he looks old enough to have heart attacks and need pills. But Mr Feinstein could see all those words in my head because he said, 'They're not poisoned.' And I picked up the Jammie Dodger and held it in my hand, but I didn't bite into it, not yet. Not until I was sure. So I asked him. Because I didn't know how else to find out without a superpower. I said, 'Why were you looking at Nan's house?' Mr Feinstein looked down, i.e. he didn't make eye contact, and I made a note in my mental logbook (which is not as good as a real one because sometimes things get rubbed out by mistake because you think of something else too quickly), but then he looked straight at me and said, 'I'm lonely. I'm a lonely old man, Billy, and I thought she might be lonely too and want to come out sometime.' And he didn't blink or fidget or go red. So

159

I said, 'She is lonely, because now Dolly is dead.' He said, 'Her cat?' I nodded. He said, 'That is sad. She has lost someone she loved. Will you tell her for me, Billy, tell her I'm sorry for her loss.' I nodded again but I had one more question just to be sure.

I said, 'What does *Ich liebe dich* mean? Is it code?' Mr Feinstein smiled. 'I love you.' And I thought he was just saying it to me that he loved me, which is weird because he doesn't know me, not really. But then he said, 'The note on the wall. It's German. It means *I love you*. My wife wrote it to me, a long time ago.' I said, 'I didn't know you had a wife.' He said, 'I don't. Not any more.' And the spy bit in me said, 'She's buried under the patio and you are next, Billy Grimshaw,' but the boy bit said, 'What happened to her?'

Mr Feinstein said, 'She died in the war, Billy. In a camp. I was there, too, but I lived. But now I'm cold all the time. Imagine that. Cold even in summer.' And I thought about what Miss Horridge said about the Holocaust, and about those pictures in the Imperial War Museum, and I felt cold too, because one of those thin women was her, Mrs Feinstein. She died because the Nazis took her away, and because no one spoke out, no one said anything. 'I'm sorry,' I said. And he nodded. And then I bit into my biscuit and it tasted sweet, of jam and shortbread. And I knew there was no poison. And he wasn't bad. He was just old and lonely, and there is nothing scary in that.

Dave wrote him a cheque for the door. I'm going to pay him back from my pocket money. It's our secret. Me, Dave and Mr A M Feinstein. We were standing on the doorstep and he bent down, not very far because he is short, shorter than Dave, and I could see everything on his face, the little holes in his skin and the lines and the hairs in his nose. But I wasn't scared, because of what he said. He said, 'Look for the good in people, Billy. Everyone has good in them. Try to see it, and make it grow.' And I knew what he meant. I knew the good was the seed. And I could feel mine growing. Because of Dave. Because of what he'd done. And what he was about to do.

When we got home Mum was sat on the sofa, and I

knew something was wrong because my rucksack was on the floor in front of her and my clothes and the *Zac Black Annual* were on the floor, and she was reading something. She was reading the logbook. And the happy seed inside me shrank down into nothing and all the good feeling from Mr Patel and Shoe Mania and Mr Feinstein evaporated like water into the air until there was nothing inside but heaviness.

She looked up and her eyes were red and I waited for her to shout and scream at me for being bad, but she didn't shout, she spoke quietly like a whisper, she said, 'I didn't know, Billy. I didn't know.' And Dave said, 'Jeanie?' But Mum didn't hear him, she just stood up and walked out of the room.

She was lying on my bed looking up at the ceiling with the logbook across her chest. I didn't say anything, I just lay down next to her and looked at the stars. After a while she said, 'Orion is missing his belt.' I said, 'I know.' But I knew that wasn't what she was thinking even though I can't read minds. I knew it was something important.

It was. She said, 'I should have seen what was

happening, Billy. I should have known. I'm your mum.' I said, 'It doesn't matter now.' But I felt her shake her head. She said, 'It does. It's too quick. It's all too quick. You're still missing him. Your dad. I should have listened to your nan.' Then I felt her face turn towards mine and her breath was on my neck all hot and I turned and could see the faded felt tip around her eyes and the redness and sadness inside them. She said, 'I won't do it, Billy. I'll cancel it. Postpone it. Until I'm ready. Until we're all ready.' And the spy bit in me said, 'You've done it, Billy! Mission accomplished.' But the boy bit didn't feel excited and pleased and victorious, it felt empty. So I didn't say 'Thanks.' Instead I said, 'Is Dave the ONE?' and I could see she thought I was mad because her forehead wrinkled up, and I knew Big Lauren would say she needs Botox, but Mum nodded anyway. I said, 'How do you know?' She said, 'I just do, Billy. You'll understand one day.' I said, 'Lauren says it's chemicals and there's nothing you can do. You're powerless.' Mum laughed then. She said, 'Something like that.' And then I thought harder than I have ever thought in my life. About Dad. Not just in London in his pants and his Radiohead T-shirt, but when he was here and he was shouting all the time and smelt of beer and forgot to come home at night and forgot my birthday. And I thought about Dave. About him carrying me out of school when I felt ill, about him driving to London to save me, about him not telling Mum, about him saving Sean Hawkes, and about the safe feeling. And I understood. And I said, 'Marry him, Mum. Tomorrow.' She said, 'Are you sure?' I said, 'He's the ONE.'

She left the logbook on my bed. But I didn't read it. I didn't even open it. I put it in the rubbish bin. Then I closed my eyes and slept.

Saturday
5th July

It was the wedding today. Stan ate three lots of trifle and was sick and Nan had to take him home. But I stayed until ten o'clock and danced with Mum.

Mum looked like Princess Leia again. The felt tip was almost gone and Stacey covered the rest with concealer. Dave didn't wear a Jedi outfit, he had a suit on just like me and Stan only bigger. Nan said he looked like Errol Flynn but I didn't know who that was so I said he looked like Zac Black at the Embassy Ball. Dave said either sounded good to him.

Nan's getting a new cat from the animal shelter.

He's ginger and called Tammy and isn't allowed to eat cornflakes. I said I thought she didn't trade her men in for a new model. She clacked her teeth a bit. Then she said, 'If they go of their own accord, maybe you just have to accept it.' So I told her about Mr A M Feinstein being lonely. She said, 'Is he German?' I said yes and I thought she was going to say something bad but she didn't. She said, 'I've always fancied Germany. They have a lot of cake.'

Big Lauren came too. She looked like a mermaid in her dress, even though it was still tight because of the big bones. And because she says she's medically addicted to Micro Chips, it's her weakness. I told her she looked amazing. And I told her that I was sorry. And at first she shrugged. But then Leona Lewis came on, and I started dancing really madly to make her laugh. And she did. She said, 'You're OK, Billy Grimshaw.' I said, 'I'm not Billy Grimshaw.' She said, 'Who are you? Zac Black?' I said, 'No, I'm still Billy. But I'm Billy Grimshaw-Jones now.'

Mum said I didn't have to. But I said I didn't mind if

it made her happy, and she said it did. But I said there's no way I am calling him Dad. He's Dave. Not mental Dave though. Just Dave.

She said that's a start.

THE LONDON MURDER MYSTERIES

The MONTGOMERY MURDER

CORA HARRISON

In the mean streets of Victorian London lies the
body of wealthy Mr Montgomery.

The police must move fast to catch his killer.
They need an insider, someone streetwise,
cunning, bold . . . someone like Alfie.

When Inspector Denham makes him an offer he
can't refuse, it's up to Alfie and his gang
to sift clues, shadow suspects and negotiate a sinister
world of double-dealing and danger
– until the shocking truth is revealed.

Secret of the Skull

SIMON CHESHIRE

What strange and sinister secret is lurking at the home of Saxby's classmate? Who is the shadowy person in need of Saxby's help, and why won't they reveal their identity? Why is the school's most notorious bully suddenly being so nice?

Solve three mind-baffling mysteries alongside Saxby Smart, schoolboy detective! Saxby reveals the clues that solve the cases but are you 'smart' enough to work out the answers?

T M Alexander

Labradoodle on the Loose

The Tribers – Bee, Jonno, Keener, Fifty
and Copper Pie – have more fun
getting in and out of adventures.

Fifty causes all sorts of mayhem when he
accidentally kidnaps his own little sister!
Keener is too busy working out how to
mountainboard to remember
he's dog-sitting Bee's Labradoodle.
Bee does a good job of forgetting her birthday,
then remembering it, and then wishing she hadn't.
It's non-stop for Tribe!

Perfect for fans of Jeremy Strong!